GRANT

IN SAINT LOUIS

GRANT

IN SAINT LOUIS

BY WALTER B. STEVENS

FROM LETTERS IN THE
MANUSCRIPT COLLECTION
of WILLIAM K. BIXBY

APPLEWOOD BOOKS
Bedford, Massachusetts

Grant in Saint Louis was originally published in 1916
by The Franklin Club of Saint Louis.

Thank you for purchasing an Applewood book.
Applewood reprints America's lively classics — books from
the past that are still of interest to modern readers.

For a free copy of our current catalog, write to:
Applewood Books
P.O. Box 365
Bedford MA 01730
or visit us on the web at:
www.awb.com

ISBN 978-1-5570-9085-0

PREFACE

In 1916 the common perception of Ulysses S. Grant's years in St. Louis, Missouri, was that of failure. Few individuals knew of his long association with the area, or his plans to retire to his St. Louis farm known as White Haven. It was in this atmosphere that Walter B. Stevens, noted journalist and author, was asked by The Franklin Club, a group of printers and publishers in St. Louis, to write a book that presented a full account of Grant in St. Louis. A collection of letters from President Grant to his farm caretaker had been made available to the Club that shed new light on his deep interest in White Haven, as well as his close association with many friends and associates in St. Louis.

Stevens used these and other letters by Grant that were available at the time, and researched newspapers, biographies, and reminiscences of him to tell the story of Grant's St. Louis connection within the larger context of his times. Stevens's book accurately refutes the misperception of Grant as a failure during the years he resided in St. Louis, but with only 100 copies printed only a small audience felt its impact.

Since White Haven was the key property that connected Grant to St. Louis, it is fitting that the National Park Service, which now administers the historic core of the estate, has brought the book out of obscurity to see its reprinting. In 2007, the site, now known as Ulysses S. Grant National Historic Site, celebrated the completion of the restoration of the five historic structures to their 1875 appearance, and the opening of an interpretive museum that places Ulysses, his wife Julia, and the many other early residents of White Haven within the larger context of 19th century American history. In some ways, what has been accomplished at the site through this restoration and interpretive development is a transformation of Stevens's book that encompasses the actual place where Grant spent so much of his time and effort, and a broader understanding of the context of his times.

It may seem strange to the average reader today that Stevens, in a book discussing Grant's association with St. Louis, would devote his longest chapter to the Whiskey Ring scandal, an event that reached national proportions. Although individuals were implicated throughout the country, the people in St. Louis who were accused of being involved were some of Grant's closest friends and acquaintances. The trials held in St. Louis were seen as especially important since President Grant was willing to come to the city and testify on behalf of his private secretary and former military aide Orville Babcock. Cabinet members persuaded Grant that such a move was ill-advised, although he did give a deposition that ultimately resulted in Babcock's acquittal. Historians are still divided as to whether or not Babcock was guilty, but all agree with Stevens' assessment that Grant was not part of the scandal, and that when informed of the abuses he wanted all guilty individuals brought to justice. Stevens' analysis, while focusing only on the St. Louis ring, accurately and incisively explains the scandal and its implications for Grant.

It is Stevens's assessment that following the Whiskey Ring scandal and trials held in St. Louis in 1875, Grant lost interest in retiring there and "'The Grant Farm' became a reminiscence" (p. xii). While this may be partially true, we now know that there were other reasons that influenced the Grants to settle in New York City after their world tour, most notably that three of their four children lived there, and the Grants, who were devoted to each other and to their children, wanted to be close to family. White Haven held many fond memories, however, and when the Grants were forced to transfer ownership of the property in 1885, Julia indicated that "it well-nigh broke my heart." (*The Personal Memoirs of Julia Dent Grant (Mrs. Ulysses S. Grant)*, p. 161)

Many of the sources that Stevens used in 1916 have also been utilized at the site, enhanced by the publication or availability of numerous other documents, articles, and books since then. This is especially true of Grant's own writings, which are being edited and published by Dr. John Y. Simon through Southern Illinois University Press, and include hundreds of papers that were unavailable to Stevens. These additional letters and papers provide further evidence that Stevens's statement, "Grant's letters reveal him," is as true today as it was in 1916 (p. ix). Stevens gave his readers the opportunity to understand Grant through his own words by quoting extensively from his memoirs and letters in *Grant in St. Louis*. Similarly, exhibits at Ulysses S. Grant National Historic Site include numerous quotes from Ulysses and Julia Grant, along with many of their contemporaries, to reveal the personal and public lives of these two individuals, who had such a long association with and deep affection for St. Louis.

We are pleased to make this important work available to the public once again.

Pamela K. Sanfilippo
Ulysses S. Grant National Historic Site Historian
St. Louis, Missouri

WALTER B. STEVENS

In the latter part of the nineteenth century Walter B. Stevens was regarded as one of America's preeminent journalists. As the Washington correspondent for the *St. Louis Globe-Democrat* from 1884 to 1901, Stevens was at the pinnacle of his profession. A Stevens's by-line guaranteed both accuracy and clarity.

Walter Barlow Stevens was born in Meridian, Connecticut, in 1848. Seven years later he moved with his family to Newton, Iowa, and a year later to Peoria, Illinois, where his father would serve as the pastor of the First Congregational Church for the next 25 years. After his preliminary education in Peoria he attended the University of Michigan, receiving a Bachelor of Arts degree in 1870 and a Master of Arts degree two years later.

Following his graduation Stevens joined the staff of the *St. Louis Times* as a reporter.
A year later he became city editor of the *St. Louis Post-Dispatch*, and in 1881 he assumed the same position with the *St. Louis Globe-Democrat*. Three years later he became head of the *Globe-Democrat*'s Washington bureau, a post he held until 1901.

Whenever Congress was not in session, Stevens used his time to travel throughout the United States, Canada, and Mexico. In his travels he gathered information that would later appear in articles in the *Globe-Democrat*, such as "Black Labor in the South," "Among the Mormons," "Silver in a Silver Country," and "Missourians One Hundred Years Ago." Like his articles on Lincoln and Grant, some of these pieces were collected and later published as books.

In 1901 Stevens became secretary of the Louisiana Purchase Exposition Company that produced the 1904 World's Fair in St. Louis. For his activities in connection with the Fair, Stevens received many honors from foreign countries. He was made a Knight of the Crown of Italy, and he received the Order of the Double Dragon of China, the Order of the Rising Sun of Japan, and the Order of the Red Eagle of Germany. He was also honored by the governments of France and Belgium.

He continued as secretary of the exposition company until all business and financial affairs were concluded in 1908. Thereafter he devoted most of his attention to historical research and writing. Among his most popular works were *A Reporter's Lincoln, A Centennial History of Missouri*, and *St. Louis: The Fourth City, 1764-1909*. He served as secretary of the St. Louis Plan Commission from

1912 to 1916, during which time he wrote *Grant in Saint Louis*. His well-received historical articles and books led to his selection as President of the State Historical Society of Missouri from 1917 to 1925.

While Stevens continued to reside in St. Louis after the Fair, he did spend several months each year on a farm that he purchased near Burdick, Kansas. About 1920 he acquired a home in Georgetown, South Carolina. Thereafter he divided his time between there and his Kansas farm, spending the summers in Kansas and the winters in South Carolina. He died at Georgetown on August 28, 1939. He was 91 years old.

John Deutch
Park Ranger
Ulysses S. Grant National Historic Site
St. Louis, Missouri

Table of Contents

Illustrations

Grant's Letters

Grant's Letters

Grant's letters reveal him. The great commander was a man of few spoken words. He avoided speeches. His Memoirs are wonderful military history, but were written while disease was preying. Of the state papers within the eight years at the White House no one can be sure how much was Grant's and how much was the secretaries'. Biographers have looked through lenses of varying power and color. His personal letters give the nearest vision and most satisfying appreciation of Grant, the man.

Two collections of these letters have been published. Grant corresponded with Elihu B. Washburne from the beginning of the Civil War to about the time the third term nomination was attempted in 1880. The letters to Washburne were made public several years ago. When Grant entered the army as colonel of an Illinois regiment in 1861, Washburne was the member of Congress from the Galena district. He had been in Congress nearly ten years and was influential. Grant moved from St. Louis to Galena in 1859 to enter the leather business with his brothers, their father supplying the capital. Washburne had faith in Grant and was his friend at Washington. The letters show that Grant realized this. They were written with utmost frankness. Mr. Washburne was in Congress not only throughout the Civil War but until 1869 when Grant, having been elected President, offered him the first place in his cabinet, Secretary of State. The position was not congenial to Washburne and he was appointed minister to France.

Grant's Letters

The second collection of Grant letters was given more recent publicity. These letters are from the farm near St. Louis, from the camp in war, from the White House and from stopping places on the journey around the world. They were written by Grant to his father, his sister and other home folks.

A third collection of Grant letters supplies the motive of this book. Some time after the war Grant came into possession of the old Dent estate on the Gravois road. There he had gone a-courting when he was a lieutenant. There he had built his first home. There his children were born. Grant employed a superintendent, improved the land and acquired blooded stock. These letters relate to "the Grant farm." They were written on White House stationery. As the President neared the close of his second term, his interest in the St. Louis farm increased. He expended money freely in his plans of improvement. Evidently he contemplated retirement to White Haven, as the estate had been known for generations. Suddenly came the Whiskey Ring exposures. They centered in St. Louis. They involved men of high official position and of influential business standing, men whom Grant had known well and looked upon as friends for many years. Some of those caught in the conspiracy sought to convey the impression that the President had connived at the frauds. Until April, 1875, Grant's strong interest in the farm was shown in his letters of instruction to his superintendent. On the 10th of May revenue officers arrived in St. Louis and seized ten *distilleries. A grand jury was called and investigation of the frauds led to many indictments. In July a relative of Mrs. Grant wrote on the stationery of the Kirkwood hotel a long letter to the President telling him of the boasts the indicted were making that he would not let them suffer. The trials had not then taken place. This letter is in the Bixby collection. On the back of it, in the handwriting of Grant, is indorsed:*

"Referred to the Sec. of the Treas. This was intended as a private letter for my information and contained many extracts from St. Louis not deemed necessary to forward. They are obtainable and have no doubt been all read by the federal officials in St. Louis. I forward this for information and to the end that if it throws any light upon new parties to summon as witnesses they may be brought out. Let no guilty man escape if it can be avoided. Be specially vigilant—or instruct those engaged in the prosecutions to be—against all who insinuate that they have high influence to protect, or to protect them. No personal consideration should stand in the way of performing a public duty."

July 29th, '75.   U. S. Grant.

Throughout that summer of 1875 the investigation went on. Indicted distillers, gaugers and storekeepers broke down and confessed. They implicated higher officials—supervisors, collectors of internal revenue, special agents, Treasury officials at Washington. Day by day the "Great Whiskey Ring" scandal was the leading news feature in the papers. Urgent pressure was brought to bear upon President Grant to retire from his Cabinet Secretary of the Treasury Bristow who was pushing the exposures. For months it was unsuccessful. In August an examination of telegraph files at St. Louis and Washington brought to light messages in the handwriting of General Orville E. Babcock, the President's secretary, signed with an assumed name and addressed to ringleaders in the conspiracy. It became public information that the grand jury was considering the fresh evidence and that the indictment of Babcock was impending.

On the 24th of September President Grant came to St. Louis. He remained four days and went on to Des Moines to attend the annual encampment of the Grand Army of the Republic. The following month Grant directed his business representative in St. Louis "to close out all his personal property, and to rent or lease out the farm and to give possession upon perfecting the lease." This was done. "The Grant Farm" became a reminiscence. Grant traveled much and made his home in the East. He seldom came to St. Louis. He took little or no more interest in White Haven.

These letters of Grant are in the manuscript collection of Mr. W. K. Bixby, through whose courtesy the Franklin Club now publishes them. They gain much interest and significance when their relationship, in point of time, with the Whiskey Ring is recalled. W. B. S.

Grant, the Boy

Grant, the Boy

Second Lieutenant Ulysses S. Grant reported for duty at Jefferson Barracks the 30th of September, 1843. Young West Pointers in that period were called upon at graduation to express their preference for branch of service; also for the regiment to which they wished to be assigned. They gave first and second choices. Grant's first choice was the dragoons, as the cavalry was then called. He missed that and was assigned to his second choice, the 4th Infantry. Notwithstanding his service was to be with a foot regiment, he brought from his Ohio home to St. Louis his horse, saddle and bridle.

Grant was called "The Tanner Boy" by one of his biographers. In his Memoirs he writes of his boyhood: "While my father carried on the manufacture of leather and worked at the trade himself, he owned and tilled considerable land. I detested the trade, preferring almost any other labor; but I was fond of agriculture and of all employment in which horses were used."

When he was seven or eight years old he drove the team which hauled wood from his father's fifty acres of forest to the house and the shops. Others loaded and unloaded, but the small boy handled the team. From the time he was eleven years old he "did all of the work that was done with horses" on the farm. As one of his compensations for the work he was allowed, occasionally, to take a horse and ride away fifteen miles to visit grandparents in an adjoining county.

Grant, the Boy

Once the boy went seventy miles with a two-horse carriage to take some people to Chillicothe and drove back alone.

He made other trips with the horses. One of these was to Flat Rock in Kentucky. At Flat Rock he saw a fine saddle horse and offered to trade for it one of his father's horses which he was driving. The owner of the saddle horse wouldn't consider the trade until he learned that the boy was allowed to do about as he pleased with the horses. Grant was then fifteen. The owner frankly said he did not know that his horse had ever had on a collar. The boy was willing to take the chance and the bargain was made. Grant got the saddler into harness and hitched him to a farm wagon for trial. It was evident that the horse had never been broken to harness, but Grant thought he could manage, and with ten dollars "boot" in his pocket started to drive the seventy miles home. He made good progress until a vicious dog jumped out in the road. The horses ran; the new one "kicked at every jump he made." The boy recovered control and stopped the team before damage was done. He thought he had quieted the horses, but as soon as he started they began kicking and running. This second runaway came to an end on the edge of a steep embankment twenty feet high, with the green horse trembling from fright. As often as Grant tried to start there was more plunging and kicking. The boy got out,

4

took a large colored handkerchief—it was called a bandana in those days—and blindfolded the horse. In this way he reached Maysville where he borrowed a driving horse from a relative and led his saddle horse the rest of the way.

"Lys" Grant was the identical boy in a horse story which has since become an American stable classic. The boy was sent to buy a colt. His father told him to offer twenty dollars first and raise to twenty-two and a half and then to twenty-five if he couldn't buy cheaper. When the boy got to the place he said to the owner: "Papa says I may offer you twenty-dollars for the colt; but if you won't take that I may offer you twenty-two and a half; and if you won't take that I may give you twenty-five." Grant was that boy. He admits it in his Memoirs:

"This story is nearly true. I certainly showed plainly that I had come for the colt and meant to have him. I could not have been over eight years old at the time. This transaction caused me great heart-burning. The story got out among the boys of the village, and it was a long time before I heard the last of it. Boys enjoy the misery of their companions, at least village boys in that day did, and in later life I have found that all adults are not free from the peculiarity. I kept the horse until he was four years old, when he went blind, and sold him for twenty dollars. When I went to Maysville to school, in 1836, at the age of fourteen, I recognized my colt as one of the blind horses working in the tread-wheel of the ferry-boat."

When Grant came home for his furlough after two years at West Point there was awaiting him a young horse that had never been in harness. The father remembered the son's favorite recreation and provided for it in this way. Two years later Grant returned home a second lieutenant of infantry. He immediately ordered his uniform. It was a time of "great suspense," he says, until he could "get in that uniform and see how it looked." He frankly admits that he wanted his old schoolmates, "particularly the girls," to see him in it. In later life Grant was thought to be rather careless of personal appearance. A picture, an old daguerreotype, taken when he was a young officer and smooth shaven gives an impression of Grant altogether different from the pictures taken during and after the war.

The young lieutenant in his brand new uniform quickly came to grief. This is another horse story and of his own telling. Soon after the suit came home from the tailor's, Grant "donned it and put off for Cincinnati on horseback." He rode slowly along the streets of the city, imagining that every one was looking at him. A little boy, bareheaded, barefooted, with trousers held up by one suspender and a shirt that had not seen a washtub for weeks, shouted shrilly to him: "Soldier! will you work? No Sir-ee; I'll sell my shirt first." Grant says: "The horse trade and its dire consequences were recalled to mind."

Grant, the Lieutenant

Grant, the Lieutenant

Extraordinary fondness for horses was one of the marked characteristics of Grant. It began in his early boyhood. It grew with him to manhood. It is shown in the series of letters this book contains. Indirectly it led to Grant's courtship and marriage. Basely it was treated as a weakness and abused in the attempt to smirch the great soldier's name.

At Jefferson Barracks in 1843, Grant was under the command of General Stephen Watts Kearny, afterwards the Mexican war hero. If the young lieutenants attended roll calls and drills punctually, they might go where they chose when off duty. Kearny required no written applications for leave. He did not care to know where the lieutenants were going or how long they intended to stay, if they returned in time for duty. To the horse, saddle and bridle brought from Ohio, Grant turned for favorite recreation. He rode out from the Barracks into the suburbs of St. Louis and soon found his way to White Haven, the home of the Dents. In Grant's class at West Point was Fred T. Dent, son of the owner of White Haven. During their last year at the Academy, Grant and Dent roomed together. The young Ohio lieutenant was welcomed. His rides to White Haven were frequent. An older daughter of the house of Dent, Miss Julia, had been at boarding school in St. Louis. She was visiting relatives, Colonel John O'Fallon's family, when Grant began his rides to White Haven.

9

Grant, the Lieutenant

After Miss Julia returned home it was noticed that the lieutenant came more frequently. There were walks and rides and visits to neighbors. Grant became well known in the Gravois community. If the 4th Infantry had remained at Barracks this situation, Grant says, "might have continued for some years without my finding out that anything was the matter with me." But in the spring of 1844, agitation over the annexation of Texas and threatened trouble with Mexico became serious. The 4th Infantry was ordered to Red River. Grant was on leave visiting his Ohio home when his regiment left. He hurried back to St. Louis, got a few days longer leave from Lieutenant Ewell, who was afterwards a famous Confederate general, mounted a horse and rode over the familiar route from the Barracks to White Haven. Gravois creek was booming. At that time there was not a bridge the entire length of the creek. Ordinarily the flow of water wasn't enough "to run a coffee mill," as Grant described it. When the lieutenant reached his usual fording place, the water was over the banks and running swiftly. Grant stopped and thought. Casually recalling that experience in his Memoirs he makes, in simple, homely expressions, a revelation of that trait which was to astound the world a few years later. When, as the general, he moved toward Richmond by the left flank and sent back word to Washington, "We will fight it out on this line if it takes all summer," he was only reiterating what he thought as he sat on his horse at the edge of unfordable Gravois creek.

"One of my superstitions had always been when I started to go anywhere, or to do anything, not to turn back, or stop until the thing intended was accomplished. I have frequently started to go to places where I had never been and to which I did not know the way, depending upon making inquiries on the road, and if I got past the place without knowing it, instead of turning back I would go on until a road was found turning in the right direction, take that, and come in by the other side."

This "superstition" was applied twenty years later when Grant tried first one route and then another to get into Vicksburg until he had completely circled the supposed impregnable stronghold of the Confederacy and compelled surrender.

He struck into the Gravois, was carried down stream, kept his horse headed to the west and climbed the other bank. But he was wet to the skin when he reached White Haven. The resourceful Miss Julia promptly produced a suit of her brother's clothes. Sitting in the borrowed garments, which were a bad fit, Grant told of the discovery he had made when he learned that he had been ordered away from Jefferson Barracks. The young lady modestly admitted that she had felt "a depression of spirits" for which she could not account when the regiment left. They parted with "an agreement." That was in May, 1844. The "agreement" continued until the 22nd of August, 1848, when it was fulfilled. During the more than four years Grant saw Miss Dent only once; that was in May, 1845, when he came back to St. Louis on a short leave and got the consent of the parents to a formal engagement.

White Haven was given its name in memory of the old home of the Dents in Maryland. The original White Haven was a grant from King Charles to the ancestors of the Frederick Dent who came to Missouri in 1815. White Haven on the Gravois road consisted of nearly 1,000 acres. Dent bought when land was cheap. It is history that one of the large estates near White Haven was acquired in the pioneer period by a trade of whiskey for land on the basis of one gallon of whiskey for each acre of ground.

Grant returned with his regiment from Mexico in the summer of 1848. He obtained four months leave of absence, came to St. Louis and was married on the 22nd of August to Miss Julia Dent, who was described in a St. Louis paper as "a lady of refinement and elegant manners." The Dents were Southerners originally but had lived for many years on the large estate southwest of the city. They owned slaves and farmed on an extensive scale. At the same time the head of the house, Colonel Frederick Dent, dealt in land claims. He acquired possession of an old Spanish claim which he tried to enforce against a considerable portion of Carondelet, afterwards annexed to St. Louis. Colonel Dent was pressing this claim at the time of the marriage and for several years after that event. He was finally defeated and took the loss with a good deal of feeling.

The marriage of Lieutenant Grant to Miss Dent took place at the Dent town house on Fourth and Cerre streets. The house was not in the most fashionable part of the city but in a very respectable locality, near the Sacred Heart convent and the French market. Chouteau avenue, with its mansions, was only a short distance. The wedding ceremony was followed by dancing which continued until midnight. Officers from the Barracks were present. One of them was Longstreet, afterwards the Confederate general. Military marriages between army officers and St. Louis girls were frequent in those days.

Grant was assigned first to Sackett's Harbor and then to Detroit. In 1852 his regiment was ordered to the Pacific Coast. Mrs. Grant and the boy, Frederick Dent Grant, who became a major-general in the United States Army and died in 1913, came to the home in St. Louis to remain until the husband and the father could arrange to have them join him in California. The 4th Infantry was ordered to Fort Vancouver on the Columbia river, where potatoes were selling at sixteen cents a pound. There Grant's knowledge of horses came into play again. The lieutenant bought a team which had crossed the plains and was very poor. Under his care the horses recuperated. While Grant broke the ground, three of his fellow officers dropped and covered the seed potatoes. This was to be a speculation that might show the way to bring out the family to the Coast. The crop flourished and promised enormous yield. Grant tells the result:

"Luckily for us the Columbia river rose to a great height from the melting of the snow in the mountains in June, and overflowed and killed most of our crop. This saved digging it up, for everybody on the Pacific Coast seemed to have come to the conclusion at the same time that agriculture would be profitable. In 1853 more than three-quarters of the potatoes raised were permitted to rot in the ground, or had to be thrown away. The only potatoes we sold were to our own mess."

On the 5th of July, 1853, Grant reached his captaincy and joined his company at Humboldt Bay, California. In 1854 he resigned from the army. He had been separated from wife and children three years. He resigned because, "I saw no chance of supporting them on the Pacific Coast out of my pay as an army officer."

In 1850 Mrs. Grant came home to St. Louis from Detroit where Grant was then stationed. Fred Dent Grant was born at St. Louis, in May of that year. He was given the name of his maternal grandfather. There was a domestic reason why Mrs. Grant did not accompany her husband when the 4th Infantry was sent rather suddenly to the Pacific Coast in June, 1852. Mrs. Grant went first to the home of her husband's people at Bethel in Ohio where, in July, Ulysses, the second son, was born. When the mother and baby were able to travel, Mrs. Grant returned to St. Louis and remained with the Dents until her husband left the army. Colonel Dent's negroes named the baby "Buckeye," because he was born in Ohio. That was shortened to Buck by which Ulysses was known even after he grew to manhood. In his family letters Grant spoke of this second son as Buck. He called him Buck to the last days. The two younger children were born in the four years on the farm; Ellen, or Nellie, as she was called later, was born in the summer of 1855, and Jesse Root, named for the paternal grandfather, was born in the winter of 1858.

There is a Jefferson Barracks tradition of Grant told to illustrate his fearlessness. The lieutenant was drilling his company when his commanding officer came by with some other officers and asked:

"Where are the rest of your men, Lieutenant?"

"Absent, by your leave, sir."

"That is not true."

Grant turned to the sergeant and told him to take command; then putting the point of his sword to the officer's breast said:

"Unless you apologize at once for this insult I will run you through."

The officer apologized. There are recollections of Grant's grit in the Gravois settlement. One night a bad man of the neighborhood became boisterous at a dance. Grant told him to be quiet. The bad man talked back. Grant kicked him out the door and into the road.

Some teamsters met Grant and a neighbor at a narrow place in the road. Grant was on the way to the mines with a load of props. The teamsters, relying on numbers and strength, crowded Grant and his companion into the ditch. Grant seized a club and with "Come on!" led the way to an attack which routed the teamsters.

In the social circle of which Jefferson Barracks was the center, Grant, during his lieutenant days, was called "the pretty little lieutenant" and "the little blue-eyed beauty." He was not only smooth-faced but he had "a clear, pink and white complexion." These descriptions do not suggest Grant the farmer, Grant the general, and Grant the President. They accord well with the historical fact that when the 4th Infantry officers got up amateur private theatricals to while away the time, they cast Lieutenant Grant for the part of Desdemona, and he played it.

Grant was a man of hardly average height, but he mounted a large horse with ease. He did it after a manner of his own. He did not climb into the saddle. He did not pull himself up with his hands. With his left foot in the stirrup and his left hand on the mane, he arose without jumping and by straightening the left leg until his body was high enough to let him swing the right leg over the back of the saddle. Then he let himself down into the seat. The movement was rapid but without spring or jolt.

The story of the Cicotte mare illustrates aptly Grant's expertness as well as enjoyment in the handling of horses. A Canadian Frenchman, David Cicotte, had a speedy little black mare to which Grant took a liking while he was stationed in Detroit. The lieutenant agreed to give Cicotte $200 for the mare if she could pace a mile in 2:55 drawing two men in a buggy. The mare did it with the owner and the lieutenant in the vehicle. Grant trained and drove the mare until she could show the back of the buggy to anything in Detroit. He sent her to St. Louis where she won $1,000 in a race. The Cicotte mare, as St. Louis horse fanciers of that generation knew her on the old Abbey track, sold for $1,400.

While Grant was at Jefferson Barracks, a young lieutenant, the mess of the 4th Infantry was presided over by Captain Robert Buchanan. This captain, a much older man, took it upon himself to be strict with the lieutenants fresh from West Point. A rule was adopted that any officer late at mess should be fined a bottle of wine. Even if the tardy one came in just after the soup was served, Buchanan imposed the penalty.

Grant was unfortunate. His frequent visits to White Haven were not always ended in time for prompt return to mess. In ten days the fine was imposed upon the lieutenant three times. The manner of the president of the mess was irritating:

"Grant, you are late, as usual; another bottle of wine, sir."

· "Mr. President, I have been fined three bottles of wine within the last ten days and if I am fined again I shall be obliged to repudiate."

"Mr. Grant, young people should be seen, not heard."

That was in 1844. In 1854, when his promotion to captain sent him from Vancouver to Fort Humboldt, Grant had to report to this same Buchanan, then lieutenant-colonel of the 4th Infantry. At Vancouver there had been congenial fellow officers. The potato crop was only one of the several business ventures of the officers. Grant and another shipped ice to California on a venture. They also tried a few shipments of cattle and pigs. There was something doing. At Fort Humboldt Buchanan made things disagreeable. He was still the strict disciplinarian, not to say martinet. He reported Grant to Washington for drinking. Notice was served on the captain that he must put his resignation in the hands of Colonel Buchanan and that it would be forwarded to Washington on the next offending. Grant declined to be put upon probation.

He offered Buchanan his unconditional resignation. This is army tradition. No mention of the action of Colonel Buchanan appears in the records at the War Department. Grant's straightforward resignation is there with the indorsement "accepted as tendered, Jefferson Davis, Secretary of War."

Another traditional version is to the effect that Colonel Buchanan found Grant under the influence of liquor one day after the latter came to Fort Humboldt and told him he must resign or stand trial. Fellow officers advised him to stand trial, but Grant decided that he would rather leave the army. As he departed he said to his friends, "Whoever hears of me in ten years will hear of a well-to-do Missouri farmer."

Grant, the Farmer

Grant, the Farmer

When Grant returned to St. Louis in the late summer of 1854 he found in his family a son whom he had never seen, born while he was on the Isthmus. Until the fall of 1858 he farmed. The biographers have given the impression that this was a period of successive failures, of depression and discouragement. They tell how Grant grew stoopshouldered and sad. The letters which Grant wrote in those years do not bear out this. In the summer of 1857 he sent this news from the farm to his home folks:

"My hard work is now over for the season with a fair prospect of being remunerated in everything but the wheat. My wheat, which would have produced from four hundred to five hundred bushels with a good winter has yielded only seventy-five. My oats were good and the corn, if not injured by frost this fall, will be the best I ever raised. My potato crop bids fair to yield fifteen hundred bushels."

As a matter of fact the potatoes turned out two hundred bushels to the acre. Another year he sent this cheerful account of prospects:

"This spring has opened finely for farming and I hope to do well; but I shall wait until the crops are gathered before I make predictions. I shall have about twenty acres of potatoes, twenty of corn, twenty-five of oats, fifty of wheat, twenty-five of meadow, some clover, Hungarian grass and other small products, all of which will require labor before they are got to market and the money realized for them."

Grant, the Farmer

In none of these letters written to members of his father's family is there note of pessimism or discouragement. There are pleasant bits of domestic news and comment, such as this:

"Little Ellen is growing very fast and talks now quite plainly. Fred does not read yet, but he will, I think, in a few weeks. Jesse R. is growing very rapidly, is very healthy and, they say, is the best looking child among the four. I don't think, however, there is much difference between them in that respect."

Jesse R. was named for the paternal grandfather. "Little Ellen" became Nellie Grant, who was married in the White House.

Years afterwards, looking back upon those years of farming in the Gravois settlement, Grant wrote that he "managed to keep along well until 1858." He gave up the farm because of a stubborn siege of fever and ague. He had suffered from this in boyhood. The ailment returned while he was farming and lasted over a year. It did not keep him in the house but it interfered with his work.

In the winter of 1854 Grant built a house on "the eighty" which her father had given Mrs. Grant. He says he "worked very hard, never losing a day because of bad weather and accomplished the object in a moderate way." The house has been called a "log cabin." It had two stories. A hall ran through the center, dividing the lower floor and making a double house. The upper floor was of sufficient height to give front

24

as well as end windows. At one end of the house was a large stone chimney opening into a fireplace wide enough to take in a log of considerable size. Although built of logs the house was much more imposing than the ordinary conception of a "log cabin." Grant did nearly all of the work. He cut the trees and hewed them square, leaving no bark or outer wood to encourage decay. He "scored" or notched the ends to make the corners fit well. That house was built sixty years ago. That it stands today in a condition of excellent preservation is the evidence of Grant's thoroughness.

When the logs were ready neighbors came to the "raisin" and brought their slaves to help. One man stood at each corner to guide the ends of the logs into the scored places. The others lifted. Grant stood at the left front corner and "carried it up," as the building phrase of that day went. One who was there recalls that those who helped were Harrison Long, Upshaw McCormick, Zeno Mackey, Thaddeus Lovejoy, Perry Sappington, Lint. Sappington, and Trip Reavis. Before sundown of the second day the walls were in place, so well had Grant prepared the logs. Grant did the rest of the work, putting on the roof and finishing the interior.

Colonel Dent gave his son a farm from the south side of the estate about the time he gave Mrs. Grant her farm. The younger Dent built a neat cottage fronting the Gravois road. He called it Wish-Ton-Wish, the Indian for Whip-Poor-Will. When Grant had completed his log house and the family moved in, the question of a name arose, following the custom of the neighborhood. Grant bestowed on his wife's farm the name of Hardscrabble, because he said it might be a hard scrabble to make a living there. Many years afterwards he walked over the farm and said, "I moistened the ground around these stumps with many a drop of sweat, but they were happy days after all." This was more than passing sentiment, for after the war, when he had means, Grant improved the farm and held it until the crash of his fortune in the Ferdinand Ward failure of 1885.

White Haven lay on both sides of Gravois creek. The Dent mansion stood in a grove of locusts and spruces. It was long and low with a two-story porch. Great stone chimneys built on the outside were at the ends of the main structure. In the rear were whitewashed quarters of the thirty slaves that Colonel Dent owned. Three-quarters of a mile south was Wish-Ton-Wish, the cottage of the younger Dent. A mile to the northwest was Hardscrabble, Grant's house, in a grove of oaks. It stood back about one hundred feet from the Ridge road. Grant hauled the stone for the cellar. He split the shingles. Colonel Dent not only gave his daughter the land but he also transferred to her three or four slaves. The negroes cut and loaded the wood which Grant hauled to the city. Neighbors took note that

Grant, the Farmer

Grant seldom rode on the loaded wagon but walked beside it with the explanation that horses had enough to draw the load without a lazy rider. Grant received four dollars a cord for the wood. He usually had customers secured in advance but occasionally waited on the Lucas market place, now Twelfth street, for a buyer.

A story which Gen. Grant enjoyed very much in after years turned on the wood selling experience. General Ben Butler and Senator Nesmith of Oregon, who had known Grant in Vancouver and who was the humorist of the Senate, were discussing the general's wonderful popularity. Butler said that Grant first touched the popular chord when he captured Fort Donelson with his unconditional surrender terms. "No," Nesmith said, gravely, "I think he first touched the popular cord when he hauled wood from his farm and sold it at full measure in St. Louis."

Grant's desire to be independent of his father-in-law was strong. It prompted him to unusual exertions. He hauled the split wood to St. Louis and sold it. He worked up the branches into "props," such as the coal miners used in their drifts to support the roof. In the southwestern suburbs of St. Louis several mines were in operation. Grant hauled the props to these mines and got five dollars a load. On the way home after one of these trips Grant stopped at a blacksmith shop and listened to a group of neighbors talking about the pitiable condition of a German farmer who had been burned out the night before. The neighbors were planning to do something. Grant listened and remarked, "I know that man; he is a good man." He took out of his pocket the five dollars received that day for the load; as he handed it to a member of the self-appointed relief committee, he said: "It is all I have. I wish it was more."

One of the recollections of the Gravois settlement is of Grant's reply when he was asked to join in a subscription movement for a new church. Farmer Grant is quoted as saying: "I am very glad to; we ought to have a comfortable place for preaching. I don't attend as much as I should, but Julia and the children do. We ought also to have a Sunday school in the neighborhood."

Grant was always a respecter of the Sabbath. A minister once remarked to him regretfully that so many of the great battles of the war were fought on Sunday. Grant said that was "very unfortunate" and, according to General Porter, gave this explanation:

"Of course it was not intentional, and I think that sometimes, perhaps, it has been the result of the very efforts which have been made to avoid it. You see, a commander, when he can control his own movements, usually intends to start early in the week so as not to bring on an engagement on Sunday; but delays occur often at the last moment, and it may be the middle of the week before he gets his troops in motion. Then more time is spent than anticipated in manoeuvering for position, and when the fighting actually begins it is the end of the week, and the battle, particularly if it continues a couple of days, runs into Sunday."

Grant observed Sunday strictly as a day of rest. He would not write any official correspondence if he could help it.

Grant had the finest team in the Gravois settlement. It was inevitable that horse stories should be associated with him in this as well as in all other periods of his life. Charles W. Ford was the local manager of the United States Express Company. He is said to have helped Grant in the selection of the team. He had been a warm personal friend of Grant at Sackett's Harbor. Horses always grew better in Grant's hands. It was not long until the neighbors began to look admiringly at the black and white span. Then stories went around about the big loads which the Grant team could haul. One day Grant started to St. Louis with sixty bushels of wheat on the wagon and got there. Sappington, the pioneer and patriarch of the neighborhood, heard the story and doubted it. He questioned Grant and the latter said: "We'll both load on sixty bushels. If I get to St. Louis without help and you don't, both loads are mine. If you get there without help and I don't, the one hundred and twenty bushels are yours." Sappington laughed and declined the wager, saying, "Well, Captain, I don't see how you do it." Many a time Captain Grant unhitched his team and helped a neighbor or a stranger whose horses had become stalled in a mud hole on the Gravois road.

Nellie Grant was born on the 4th of July. Year after year during her childhood her father pretended to consider that the salutes and fireworks were in celebration of her birthday. Nellie was only a baby when her father taught her to ride on the saddle with him. A rough and tumble wrestling match with his growing boys was a frequent form of home amusement. Grant indulged in it even after he became a general. Those who saw these evidences of the father's love of companionship with his family realized what the long parting while he was on the Pacific Coast must have meant to him.

A letter that came to St. Louis while Grant was "at the front" in Mississippi illustrated the strong family tie of the Grants: "Tell the children to learn their lessons, mind their grandma and be good children. I should like very much to see them. To me they are all obedient and good. I may be partial but they seem to me to be children to be proud of."

Mrs. Dent, the mother-in-law, thought a great deal of Grant and showed it in many ways. Mrs. Grant's home name for her husband was "Ulyss." She called him "Mr. Grant" before strangers, even after he became lieutenant-general. A very few intimates heard her pet name of "Victor" given after the capture of Vicksburg.

Grant, the Farmer

"Those were happy days in the log house," Mrs. Grant said after the eight years in the White House and the trip around the world. Her son, General Fred. Dent Grant, visited the log house on the World's Fair grounds when he was in St. Louis for the dedication in 1903. He went through the rooms, telling with emotion his recollections. He showed the room up stairs to the right of the middle door where he and his little brothers slept. He described the long winter evenings when the captain and Mrs. Grant sat with the children in a semi-circle in front of the blazing fire-place. He remembered that his father told of the campaign in Mexico. He had vivid recollection of what his father said of his homesickness on the Pacific Coast and of his great desire to get home and see wife and children.

No member of the Grant family looked back upon that farm life as it has been presented by some of the biographers. There was none of that poverty which has been pictured to heighten the contrast with the fame that came later. There was plenty to eat. There was social life. The captain and Mrs. Grant went out to the neighborhood gatherings; they had no light vehicle but both were good riders and each took a child on the horse. Grant did not dance but he played cards well. Checkers was his favorite game. At the shooting matches of the neighborhood, the captain held his own and got the prize, a quarter of beef, about as often as any of the neighbors.

Grant, the Farmer

Grant was popular with his neighbors along the Gravois road. He had no quarrels. To this day is remembered the way in which his sense of justice settled a difference with two neighbors. Soon after Grant went on the farm there was a misunderstanding as to the amount he was to pay Trip Reavis and Jonah Sappington for a quantity of cordwood. The two neighbors claimed more was due than Grant thought he was to pay. The captain proposed arbitration; Sappington and Reavis to appoint one arbitrator; he to appoint another; the cost of the decision of the arbitrators to be paid by the loser. Reavis and Sappington named Ben Lovejoy as their arbitrator. The captain immediately said Lovejoy would suit him, too, and that whatever the decision he would accept it. Lovejoy decided that Reavis and Sappington were right. Grant at once paid the bill.

There is a sequel to this incident. Most of those who were neighbors to Grant in his farming days owned slaves or from old associations sympathized with the South. In the settlement was formed an organization to extend aid to Confederates. Grant came up to St. Louis in January, 1862, and in accordance with his custom went out to the farm to see his father-in-law. He went about among the neighbors. Some one proposed that the organization kidnap him and take him South a prisoner. The suggestion was promptly vetoed by the leaders.

One of the traditions well preserved in the

Grant, the Farmer

Gravois neighborhood tells how Grant dealt with a neighbor who did not keep the eighth commandment. The Grant family was at that time living in Wish-Ton-Wish while the brother-in-law was away. The Hardscrabble woodlot was nearly two miles away to the north. Grant discovered that somebody was stealing wood at night. He went on guard, selecting a bright moonlight night when he thought conditions were likely to encourage the thief. He had not been watching long when a team was driven up within three or four rods of where he was hidden. The man was recognized as a renter in the vicinity. Grant waited until the wagon was loaded and the team had been driven nearly to the road; then he stepped in front and hailed. The conversation, according to tradition, was about as follows:

"Hullo, Bill! Going to St. Louis with that wood?"

"Yep."

"How much are you asking for it?"

"About four dollars."

"Well, I'll take it. Bring it over to the house."

"Nope. Promised it to a man in town."

"I must have it. You haul this load to my house, and pay me twenty dollars for what you have cut and hauled away. That won't be more than half price, you know."

"What will you do if I don't; sue me before the squire?"

"No, we won't trouble the squire or the public. We'll settle right here."

Grant, the Farmer

As the story goes, Grant dropped his humorous manner, jumped forward and grabbed the thief who was much the larger of the two. "Hold on," the fellow called, "I'll do it, but don't tell anybody." The wood was unloaded at Grant's house, the twenty dollars were paid and the incident was closed. Grant missed no more wood.

Longstreet was one of the officers from Jefferson Barracks who attended the wedding of Lieutenant Grant and Miss Dent at the town house of the Dents. He recalled the last meeting with his old comrade in St. Louis before they came together at Appomattox. It was in 1858:

"I was in St. Louis on business and there met a number of old army chums. It was a cold dreary day and a game of brag was proposed as most likely to recall old memories. We were one hand short when my friend Captain Holloway went out to find some one. He soon returned with a civilian poorly dressed in the garb of a farmer. We recognized our old friend Grant, who had resigned from the service a few years before and was at the time making an unsuccessful battle for existence in civil life. The next day, while I was standing in front of the Planter's Hotel, Grant stepped up and placed a five-dollar gold piece in my hand. He said it was a debt of honor from our association in the old Texas days.

" 'I will not take it,' said I. 'You are now out of service and need it.'

" 'But you must take it,' Grant insisted, with

34

determination, 'I will not have what does not belong to me.'

"Seeing that he was thoroughly in earnest, and to save him from mortification, I accepted it, and shaking hands, we parted. Is it any wonder that I hoped to meet him again after he had become a great general. But we never met after our parting on the steps of the Planter's Hotel in St. Louis until after the surrender. I was one of the Confederate commissioners to arrange the details of the capitulation. General Grant treated us with great kindness. He acted as though nothing whatever had happened to mar the relations which existed in the long ago by the camp fires in Texas and Mexico. As we stepped aside after the formalities, he put his arm in mine and the first thing he said to me was:

" 'Pete,' (my army sobriquet) 'let us return to the happy old days by playing another game of brag.' "

General Frederick Dent Grant's recollections of the life in St. Louis were widely at variance with the biographers. He denied with emphasis that his father was gloomy and dispirited in the years that were spent in the house of logs. He remembered him as energetic and cheerful. On one occasion not long before he died, the son said of the farm:

"I remember it very distinctly. Indeed my memory begins with the transfer of my father from the post in Detroit. When my father was ordered to go to California, my mother and I were to live in St. Louis until he established a home and sent for us. But his pay was small, flour was twenty-five cents a pound, and we remained with my grandfather. While I was playing on the long porch at White Haven, the home of my mother's family, late in the summer of 1854, a man drove up in a buggy. Just as he was throwing the lap-robe over the dashboard a colored woman ran out of the house and said: 'It's Mr. Grant.' And so it was, but I didn't know him. It is very likely he didn't know me. He had resigned his commission because he couldn't support his family if he stayed in the army. My mother had a farm, about a hundred acres, I suppose, and my father, who was an industrious and stirring man, built a log house, cutting the trees and hewing them himself. Now bear in mind that my father had graduated from West Point, had served in the Mexican war and had been an officer in the United States army, yet he sacrificed his career as he thought, and took up his work in the wilderness, that he might have a home of his own and not be under obligations to Mr. Dent, his father-in-law."

Grant "was a failure as a farmer," according to the biographers, and yet it is an historical fact that when Dent, the brother-in-law, went to California, he got Grant to take charge of Wish-Ton-Wish and run the place. It is another fact that, after Mrs. Dent, the mother-in-law, died in 1856 or 1857, Colonel Dent moved to town and turned over White Haven with the thirty slaves and all to Grant to manage for him. In September, 1858, Grant wrote home: "Julia and I are both sick with chills and fever; Freddy so dangerously ill that I thought I would not write until his fate was decided."

The next month, October, Grant told his father of the decision reached in regard to the farm, in view of the continued illness of the family: "Mr. Dent and myself will make a sale this fall and get clear of all the stock on the place and then rent out the cleared land and sell about 400 acres of the north end of the place. As I explained to you this will include my place. I shall plan to go to Covington in the spring."

The day before Christmas, 1858, Grant went into a St. Louis pawnshop and left his silver watch. He borrowed twenty dollars on it. His application for the appointment to a minor county office had failed. The temporary clerkship at the custom house had come to an end. A plan to freight goods over the Santa Fe trail had not come to anything. Months of malaria in the family had been expensive. A little ready money was needed for the Christmas season. The pawn ticket was preserved as a curiosity. After Grant died, an admirer of the general paid fifteen dollars for the scrap of paper. There is another Grant document of the same period. It is in striking contrast with the pawn ticket. Three months after he got the loan of twenty dollars on the watch to give his family a cheerful Christmas, Grant presented himself in the St. Louis Circuit Court and formally freed the only slave he ever owned. He filed this deed of emancipation:

"Know all persons by these presents that I, Ulysses S. Grant, of the City and County of St. Louis, in the State of Missouri, for divers good and valuable considerations me hereunto moving, do hereby emancipate and set free from slavery my negro man William, sometimes called William Jones, of mulatto complexion, aged about thirty-five years, and about five feet, seven inches in height, and being the same slave purchased by me of Frederick Dent. And I do hereby manumit, emancipate and set free said William from slavery forever.

"In testimony whereof I hereto set my hand and seal at St. Louis this 29th day of March, A. D. 1859."

U. S. Grant.

Grant, the Business Man

Grant, the Business Man

When the farm was given up Colonel Dent advised his son-in-law to go into the real estate business. He proposed partnership with Harry Boggs, a relative. Boggs was a real estate agent in a small way. The firm of Boggs & Grant was formed in the beginning of 1859. Deskroom was taken in the law offices of McClelland, Hillyer & Moody. These offices were on the first floor of a building which had been a residence. The location was on Pine street midway between Second and Third streets. The three lawyers and the two real estate men occupied what had been the double parlors in the days when the residence district was east of Fourth street. In March, Grant wrote to his father, "I can hardly tell you how the business I am engaged in will turn out, but I believe it will be something more than a support." He sent some of the cards of Boggs & Grant and asked his father to distribute them among such friends in Ohio as might have business in St. Louis, "such as buying and selling property, collecting either rents or other liabilities." The family had moved into town. "We are living in the lower part of the city, full two miles from my office," Grant wrote in one of his letters home. "The house is a comfortable little one, just suited to my means. We have one spare room and also a spare bed in the children's room, so that we can accommodate any of our friends that are likely to come."

The home to which Grant referred was on

Ninth and Barton streets. It was a cottage with a steep roof and large shade trees overhanging. This property was acquired by trading the Hardscrabble farm. There was a mortgage on the city place, which the seller agreed to take care of when it fell due. In the exchange Grant received a note for $3,000. He wrote home: "If I could get that cashed I would build two houses that would pay $40 a month rent." This was in 1859 while he was in the real estate business. The letter conveyed a glimpse of fatherly pride: "Fred and Buck go to school every day. They never ask to stay at home."

While the trade of Hardscrabble looked well on its face the sequel was litigation and loss. The man who sold the house and agreed to take care of the mortgage didn't do so. Grant sued for the return of Hardscrabble. The lawsuit dragged along several years.

To Harry Boggs Grant explained the idea of his father-in-law about the real estate business in this way: "The old gentleman is trying to persuade me to go into business with some one, and he speaks of you. He thinks I could soon learn the details, and that my large acquaintance among army officers would bring enough additional customers to make it support both our families."

Grant had driven in from the farm with a load of corn to sell when he had this conversation. Boggs answered: "I have worked hard to build it up and I do not want a partner unless he can increase, but I think you can. Come and see me next time you are in town."

Mrs. Boggs was a niece of Colonel Dent. She had been present at the wedding of Lieutenant Grant and her cousin Julia Dent. She favored the partnership, arranging that Grant should have the use of an unfurnished room in the house where the Boggs family lived, No. 209 South Fifteenth street, until he moved Mrs. Grant and the children in from the farm. Grant put in a bedstead with one mattress and a washbowl on a chair. He did not go to the expense of a carpet. In that room he slept during the months of January and February, 1859, walking out to the farm Saturday evenings to spend Sunday with the family.

Colonel Dent had some ground for his reference to the large acquaintance of his son-in-law with army officers. All of the time that Grant was farming he kept up friendly relations with his army friends. He was at the Barracks frequently. He called upon army men who were transient visitors in St. Louis. He had no false shame about his dress. General Beale recalled a meeting with Grant at the Planter's House. Beale was sitting outside on the pavement when Grant came along with a whip in his hand. He asked him what he was doing. Grant replied that he was "farming on a piece of land belonging to Mrs. Grant, some ten miles out in the country."

43

While they were talking the dinner bell rang as was the custom even in the best St. Louis hotel in those days. Grant started to go but Beale said:

"Come in and have dinner with me."

"Well, I don't know," was Grant's reply. "I am not dressed for company."

"That doesn't matter, come in," Beale urged. And Grant went in not at all abashed by the curious looks.

General Coppee, who had been with Grant at West Point had an even more interesting experience with him: "Grant, with his whip in his hand, once came to see me at the hotel where were Joseph J. Reynolds, then a professor, D. C. Buell and other officers. I remember that to our invitation to join us at the bar, he said: 'I will go and look at you; but I never drink anything myself.'"

To these army friends who had known him at West Point, or when he was a lieutenant he was "Sam" Grant, the name they had bestowed upon him in cadet days. Boggs found that instead of the army acquaintance being of much value it was sometimes a drawback. Grant undertook the collection of rents. If he had a bill against somebody he had known in the army he might light his cigar and sit down for an afternoon's chat on old times, forgetting about the bill in his pocket.

The partnership of Boggs & Grant made a fairly encouraging start, notwithstanding that the junior partner's chills continued through the spring months. On the suggestion of Colonel Dent, Boggs added money loaning to the business. He turned over the renting and collecting to Grant while he went East and made arrangement to handle a large sum of money for Philadelphians. The interest then obtainable in St. Louis was about twice the prevailing rate in the Quaker city

Mrs. Boggs, who had favored the partnership and who, as was the case with all other women, liked Grant, said: "He was always a gentleman and everybody loved him, he was so gentle and considerate. But really we did not see what he could do in the world."

Occupying what had been a hall bedroom in the old residence where Boggs & Grant had their real estate office was a young law student. He had come over from Belleville and was permitted to read law books in the office of Sloss & Jones, sleeping in the office at night. For his meals the young man depended upon earnings as a "sub" in a newspaper office. He was destined to become the leading criminal lawyer of St. Louis and a prominent figure in politics but he didn't know it at that time. He was satisfied to be the champion of the "Free Democrats," an organization of young St. Louisans. Between the captain and the law student developed a friendship. Each seems to have recognized in the other something that drew. Grant, when the reserve was broken,

liked to talk of his Mexican campaign and also
of politics. The young law student was an eager
listener. The two spent much time together.
There was another bond of interest between them.
It had its origin in the cold weather. An old colored woman who cleaned the offices had a room
in the rear. She wore a red bandana turban after
the manner of oldtime slaves. Her husband, a
grizzled and bent old fellow, had worked hard
and purchased his freedom. He still drove a dray.
The colored woman was more than a janitress.
She took it upon herself to "mammy" her people.
She was especially watchful over the student for
he was no more than a boy, and also over the
captain for the fever and chills still hung on, making him so weak sometimes that he had to be
helped to the street cars when he started home.
The old colored woman kept a pot of coffee on the
stove cold days. "Come in, chile," she would say
to the captain and the law student, "and get a
cup of coffee before you go out." Ten years later,
nearly, Charles P. Johnson, who had achieved
fame in his profession and was one of the political
leaders in St. Louis, went on to Washington to
see the grand review after Appomattox. He
called at the Grant residence to pay his respects
to the lieutenant-general. The two looked at each
other curiously. Grant said, "I think I know
you. Weren't you a student of law in St. Louis?"
Johnson said: "You were in the real estate business on Pine street." "Well," said the lieutenant-

general, "I am very glad to see you. Come and sit on the lounge and tell me something about the old crowd." Governor Johnson recalls the conversation which followed:

"For nearly an hour he talked with interest and animation about the various persons he had met in and around the old office on Pine street. The first question he asked, with apparent feeling, was about the old colored woman. And when I told him she had been gathered to her rest a year or two before, he expressed his sorrow and eulogized her for her many kind and amiable qualities. That old aunty had not only given us coffee in cold weather. She had sewed on buttons and mended clothes for us. Grant was a great smoker in those days on Pine street. He used both pipes and cigars. He would occasionally sit on the steps in front of his office during summer evenings and smoke and talk on various subjects. Right across the street was a cigar store kept by a thin, sharp visaged German whose complexion was yellow enough to remind one of a shriveled and dried up leaf of Virginia plant. He was good natured, quiet, talkative and afforded his customers a good deal of amusement by the novel manner in which he constructed sentences and pronounced the English language. Grant was a customer at the shop and keenly enjoyed a talk with him. The old German tobacconist was not forgotten in our talk at Washington. Grant laughed when referring to his humorous characteristics. From this he branched off into some recollections of his life in St. Louis, but resumed again as we parted his memories of the old aunty. During the entire conversation his mind seemed centered upon the recollections connected with the Pine street office and the characters to which I have alluded."

Before the summer of 1859 was ended both Boggs and Grant realized that the firm was not getting enough business to support their families. "Our present business," Grant explained to his father, "is entirely overdone in this city, at least a dozen new houses having started about the time I commenced. I do not want to fly from one thing to another nor would I, but I am compelled to make a living from the start, for which I am willing to give all of my time and energy." This comes about as near a tone of discouragement as appears in any of Grant's letters of that period.

The year 1859 was the ebb of Grant's fortunes. And yet in that year he did not sell, he emancipated the slave he had acquired from his father-in-law. He went into the St. Louis Circuit Court and filed the deed of freedom for William Jones. The paper was drawn up in the real estate office. The witnesses were McClelland and Hillyer, the lawyers with whom Grant had deskroom. "Grant did not seem to be just calculated for business," one of these lawyers said, "but a more honest, generous man never lived, I don't believe."

While he was a business man in St. Louis Grant

undertook to sell a horse for his brother Simpson who was carrying on the father's business at Galena. In October, 1859, he reported progress in this way:

"I have been postponing writing to you, hoping to make a return for your horse, but as yet have received nothing for him. About two weeks ago a man spoke to me for him and said he would try him next day and, if he suited, give me $100 for him. I have not seen the man since; but one week ago last Saturday he went to the stable and got the horse, saddle and bridle, since which I have not seen man nor horse. From this I presume he must like him. The man I understand lives in Florissant, about twelve miles from this city."

Grant wrote about other matters. After signing his name it occurred to him that he had better reassure Simpson about the horse. He added a postscript:

"The man that has your horse is the owner of six three-story brick houses in this city, and the probabilities are he intends to give me an order on his agent for the money when the rents are due."

Among those with whom Grant consulted when he knew he must find something better than the real estate business was J. J. Reynolds, afterwards a general of fame. The two were classmates at West Point. Reynolds had left the army three years previously and was professor of

mechanics and of engineering in the faculty of
Washington University, but recently organized.
He suggested the possibility of appointment to
the chair of mathematics. Nothing would have
pleased Grant better at that time. Mathematics
had been his favorite study at West Point. He
had the mathematical turn of mind as was shown
in his way of keeping accounts and even in his
recreation, for he was fond of problems which
required figuring. He had always believed he
would like teaching. While he was a lieutenant
on duty at Jefferson Barracks, within a year after
graduation, he wrote to Professor Church, who
had the chair of mathematics at the Academy,
asking that he be designated as assistant when a
detail was made. The custom was to detail young
officers from the army as assistant professors.
Church, remembering Grant's interest in mathematics while a cadet, answered encouragingly.
Grant always believed he would have gone to
West Point as assistant to Professor Church in a
year or two if the Mexican war had not come
on. "It was never my intention," he says in his
Memoirs, "to remain in the army long, but to prepare myself for a professorship in some college."

Upon the professorship of mathematics in
Washington University Grant looked longingly
but not hopefully as his correspondence written
at the time makes plain. He did not believe it
was within his reach and when the appointment
of another was made he wrote:

Grant, the Business Man

"The Washington University, where the vacancy was to be filled, is one of the best endowed institutions in the United States and all the professorships are sought after by persons whose early advantages were the same as mine but who have been engaged in teaching all their mature years. Quimby, who was the best mathematician in my class and who was for several years an assistant at West Point, and for nine years a professor in an institution in New York, was an unsuccessful applicant. The appointment was given to the most distinguished man in his department, and an author. His name is Shorano."

Grant wrote the name from hearsay. He had heard of Professor Chauvenet.

This was in August, 1859. That same month Grant made formal application to the commissioners of St. Louis county for a position. In his letter he asked for the appointment of county engineer. Technically the place was that of county superintendent of roads. The salary was $1,500. With his application Grant filed a petition headed by Thomas E. Tutt and signed by thirty well-known and substantial citizens. He wrote to the commissioners:

"I beg leave to submit myself as an applicant for county engineer, should the office be rendered vacant, and at the same time to submit the names of a few citizens who have been kind enough to recommend me for the office. I have made no effort to get a large number of names, nor the names of persons with whom I am not personally acquainted. I enclose herewith also a statement from Professor Reynolds, who was a classmate of mine at West Point, as to qualifications. Should your honorable body see proper to give me the appointment, I pledge myself to give the office my entire attention and shall hope to give general satisfaction."

Could it have been put better? The accompanying indorsement by Professor Reynolds read:
"Captain U. S. Grant was a member of the class at the Military Academy which graduated in 1843. He always maintained a high standing, and graduated with great credit, especially in mathematics and engineering. From my personal knowledge of his capacity and acquirements, as well as of his strict integrity and unremitting industry, I consider him in an eminent degree qualified for the office of county engineer."

On the same sheet of paper with Professor Reynolds' statement was another indorsement, remarkable in view of subsequent events. It was from D. M. Frost who commanded at Camp Jackson and who afterwards joined the Confederacy. Frost wrote in Grant's behalf:
"I was for three years in the corps of cadets at West Point with Captain Grant, and served with him for some eight or nine years in the army, and can fully indorse the foregoing statement of Professor Reynolds."

Under the procedure the application was

referred to the commissioner in whose district the applicant lived for a report upon it. That commissioner was Dr. William Taussig of Carondelet. Dr. Taussig had been mayor of Carondelet and had taken an active part opposing a land claim which old Colonel Dent was pressing against a considerable section of the city. He also attended the children of Grant while Mrs. Grant was with her relative, Mrs. Barnard, who lived in Carondelet. This professional service was rendered while Grant was in California. In his recollections, preserved by the Missouri Historical Society, Dr. Taussig says:

"Though we saw each other often and knew each other very well, as men in small communities do even when there is no occasion for personal contact, I never had occasion beyond bowing, to speak to General Grant until after he was President. I saw him frequently haul many of the now historic carts of cord wood for sale in St. Louis past my home and office. There was a blacksmith shop opposite me and I can see him now as he then appeared, sitting on a log in front of the shop—a serious dignified man, with slouched hat, high boots, and trousers tucked in, smoking a clay pipe and waiting for his horses to be shod.

"Nor did I ever set foot on the Dent farm, although all of the neighbors around it were my close friends, with whom I frequently visited. The old gentleman did not feel kindly toward me on account of the land suit and because I was a pronounced Republican and Union man. I always at that time had the impression that this feeling—meaning the political one—had been shared by Grant. In this, as events have shown, I was mistaken.

"The only member of the Grant family with whom I was intimate was William Barnard whose wife was a relative of Mrs. Grant. Barnard was a wholesale druggist, an amiable, jovial man, very fond of hunting, and his yard and garden were filled with wooden and cast-iron effigies of stags, deer and hunting dogs. He was too fond of good living to succeed in business, and failed early during the war. Grant, during his Presidency, made him bank examiner for Missouri under the national banking law.

"At the Barnard home I met Mrs. Grant frequently when she made some of her prolonged visits to her relative, and occasionally was called to attend her children. Both Mrs. Grant and Mrs. Barnard were charming, cultivated ladies, devoted to their husbands and children. A family physician gets to hear much that is kept from the general public, and the, to say the least, dependent position which Grant occupied in the house of his father-in-law was frequently commented upon in my presence."

With this explanation of his relations to the Grant and Dent families, Dr. Taussig leads up to the explanation of Grant's failure to receive the appointment of superintendent of county roads. He says:

"It stands in evidence of Grant's dignified pride that, hard pressed as he was at the time, he never called either on me or on any one of my colleagues in support of his application. Many strong letters from prominent people of both parties, recommending him, came to me. My old and lifelong friend, Henry T. Blow, an ardent Union man, urged me personally to recommend and support Grant for the position. Much stress was laid on his needs, his character and qualifications not being questioned. It was a perplexing position for me. Everybody knows how portentously already the clouds of disunion darkened the political horizon of the country in the latter part of 1859. Then, already, in St. Louis, the disloyal 'minute men' on the one side, and the loyal 'wide awakes' on the other, were closing ranks, and every issue, social or political, was decided or acted upon as it affected this all-absorbing question. The Dents, at least the old gentleman, were known to be pro-slavery Democrats, and to use the harsh language of that period, outspoken rebels. Grant lived with them, and though nothing was known of his political views, the shadow of their disloyalty necessarily fell upon him. We felt bound, foreseeing events to come, to surround ourselves with officers whose loyalty to the Union was unquestioned. Our court consisted of John H. Lightner, Benjamin Farrar, Col. Alton R.

Grant, the Business Man

Easton, Peregrine Tibbets and myself. Easton and Tibbets were Democrats. Col. Easton was a Union Democrat, an ex-officer of the Mexican war and had known Grant. Tibbets, a most excellent gentleman, was a pro-slavery Democrat. I made my report adverse to Grant verbally."

By a divided vote the commissioners elected Mr. Salomon, brother of Salomon, the war governor of Wisconsin. Grant, in his Memoirs, says: "My opponent had the advantage of birth over me—he was a citizen by adoption—and carried off the prize." This was a bit of sarcasm on the part of Grant. That he understood the other and real explanation of his defeat is apparent from his correspondence with his father at the time. In August, when the appointment was pending, he wrote that the board of commissioners was composed of three free soilers and two opposed, adding: "Although friends who are recommending me are the very best citizens of this place and members of all parties, I fear they will make strictly party nominations for all the offices under their control." But a more significant and important letter was sent by Grant after the appointment of Salomon. In it he defined his political status. The letter was written in September, 1859. Grant said:

"The Democratic commissioners voted for me and the Free Soilers against me. You may judge from the result of the action of the county commissioners that I am strongly identified with the

Grant, the Business Man

Democratic party. Such is not the case. I never voted an out-and-out Democratic ticket in my life. I voted for Buchanan for President to defeat Fremont, but not because he was my first choice. In all other elections, I have universally selected the candidates that, in my estimation, were the best fitted for the different offices, and it never happens that such men are all arrayed on one side. The strongest friend I had on the board of commissioners is a Free Soiler, but opposition between parties is so strong that he would not vote for anyone, no matter how friendly, unless at least one of his own party would go with him."

Grant voted for Buchanan in 1856. He had been to the city with a load of wood. On the way back to the farm he passed the country polling place and went on as if not intending to stop. But before driving far, he turned his team to a tree, tied the horses, went back and voted. It is tradition in the neighborhood that Grant then remarked he was "voting against Fremont." At the same time, however, he voted for Henry C. Wright, who was on the other side. Wright was running for the legislature. He was a Whig. He was the miller to whose place Grant went nearly every week with a bag of grain to be ground. After casting his ballot, Grant turned to Wright who was at the polling place and said: "Mr. Wright, I have voted for you today, not on the ground of politics, for I am a Democrat, but because I think you are the best man for the place."

Grant, the Business Man

Grant's comment in his Memoirs that his opponent had the advantage of birth over him was not wholly a pleasantry, although he realized that politics was the main issue. In his letter to his father Grant wrote: "There is, I believe, but one paying office in the county held by an American, unless you except the office of sheriff, which is held by a Frenchman who speaks little English, but was born here."

F. W. Mathias recalled that after the defeat for the office of superintendent of county roads, Grant remarked to a friend one day: "No American can get anything in this town." While he was on the farm Grant joined a Native American lodge. But he attended only one meeting. The Native Americans were very strong in St. Louis at that time. They were called Know Nothings, from that provision in the sworn ritual which required a member when asked by an outsider about the principles and purposes of the order to answer, "I know nothing."

Grant's ill success with the county commissioners in October did not deter him from making a second effort. In the archives of the Missouri Historical Society is the original of this letter:

St. Louis, Feb. 13, 1860.

Hon. J. H. Lightner,
    Pres. Board of County Commissioners.

Sir: Should the office of County Engineer be vacated by the will of your honorable body, I would respectfully renew the application made by me in August last for that appointment. I would also, by leave, refer to the application and recommendations then submitted and now on file with your board. I am sir,

Respectfully your obt. svt.,

U. S. Grant.

In October, after the county commissioners had acted adversely on his application, Grant wrote home that his name had been forwarded for the appointment of superintendent of the custom house. "I am still unemployed," he said, "but expect to have a place in the custom house from the first of next month." He explained that if he was not appointed superintendent he was to get a desk as clerk in the custom house. He did receive the clerkship, but it lasted only about a month.

When nothing came of his second application to the county commissioners in February, 1860, Grant decided to go to Galena where his brothers, Simpson and Orville, were running their father's leather store. Most of Grant's biographers have held to the view that Grant was given the clerkship in the Galena store as a matter of charity on the part of the rest of the family. The fact was that the father, Jesse Root Grant, was planning to establish his three sons in business by turning over to them this leather store. Grant went up to Galena in 1856 and visited his brothers, but was not ready to join them. He preferred the Hardscrabble farm. Jesse Root Grant was a man of original ideas. He had accumulated a good fortune for that period. He had three sons and three daughters and he proposed to make the sons independent with their own help. For years he had been announcing his intention to retire from active business when he was sixty. His plan, in 1860, as described by Frederick Dent Grant, was very different from that told by the biographers and historical novelists. It was this:

"My grandfather, Jesse R. Grant, was then living in Covington, Ky. He owned tanneries at Portsmouth on the Ohio river, had a large leather store at Galena, in Illinois; a branch store at LaCrosse, in Wisconsin, and, I think, another store somewhere in Iowa. My Missouri grandfather—and he owned an estate of many hundreds of acres himself—thought my Ohio or Kentucky grandfather a rich man. 'Old Mr. Grant,' I once heard him say, 'must be worth $150,000.' Anyway my Grandfather Grant was advancing in years and wanted to distribute his property. It was arranged that my father and his two brothers should manage the tanneries and stores, each to be paid $60 a month for his services, and place the profits of the business in a trust fund for their three sisters. When the accumulated profits amounted to the value of the tanneries and stores the brothers were to have the physical property and the sisters the income from the money in trust. We moved to Galena and took a good house. I recall that I was disgusted because I couldn't go barefooted like other boys and that instead of a hickory shirt and one suspender I had to wear a waist which I buttoned to my short trousers. The store building in Galena was four stories high, and was packed with goods. Behind it was the harness factory which extended to the next street. There was also a large stock of carriage hardware. Father has said that he was a clerk in those days, but he was much more; in time he would have been a partner in the business. I recollect that his salary of $60 a month was less than he really required, and that several gifts of money to my mother from her family in St. Louis helped him considerably. The largest, I think, was about $100. Grandfather Grant was at no time a liberal man. We lived in Galena eleven months and then my father went away to the war. He talked rather freely in the family as soon as it was known that Lincoln had been elected, and he predicted that some of the Southern states would secede. The Dents in St. Louis were rebels. He wrote to them, expressing his sympathy, regretting the coming conflict, but telling them that the South would be whipped. In the evening of the day on which Lincoln made his first call for troops, a public meeting was held in Galena, at which father presided. He never went to the leather store after that meeting to put up a package or do any other business."

Grant went to Galena in May, 1860, and joined his two brothers in the management of the store, accepting his father's plan. As he was less familiar with the business than the others he took what might be considered a subordinate position so far as duties were concerned. He continued in the store eleven months and then joined the army. The war interfered with the plan of partnership. In 1866 Jesse Root Grant was ready to distribute a considerable part of his estate, about $100,000, among his children. General Grant refused to take his share saying he had helped to make none of his father's wealth. The general's children were given $1000 each by their grandfather.

Grant, the General

Grant, the General

From Galena Grant wrote a remarkable letter to his father-in-law in St. Louis. It was the day after he had presided at a meeting in April, 1861, to raise a company of volunteers for the war. Grant realized that he was going into service. He had said as much in a letter to his father. He was face to face with the question of what Mrs. Grant and the four children should do, and he proceeded to put the situation before "the old gentleman" as he called Mrs. Grant's father:

"All party distinction should be lost sight of, and every true patriot be for maintaining the glorious stars and stripes, the constitution and the Union. The North is responding to the President's call in such a manner that the Confederates may truly quake. I tell you there is no mistaking the feelings of the people. The government can call into the field 75,000 troops and ten and twenty times 75,000 if it should be necessary, and find the means of maintaining them, too. It is all a mistake about the northern pocket being so sensitive. In times like the present no people are more ready to give of their time or of their abundant means.

"No impartial man can conceal from himself the fact, that in all these troubles the Southerners have been the aggressors, and the administration has stood purely on the defensive, more on the defensive than she would have dared to have done, but for her consciousness of right prevailing in the end.

"The news today is that Virginia has gone out of

the Union. But for the influence she will have on the border states, this is not much to be regretted. Her position, or rather that of eastern Virginia has been more reprehensible from the beginning than that of South Carolina. She should be made to bear a heavy portion of the burden of the war for her guilt.

"In all this I can see but the doom of slavery. The Northerners do not want, nor will they want, to interfere with the institution, but they will refuse for all time to give it protection unless the Southerners shall return soon to their allegiance; and then, too, this disturbance will give such an impetus to the production of their staple—cotton —in other parts of the world that they can never recover the control of the market again for that commodity. This will reduce the value of the negroes so much that they will never be worth fighting over again."

To these general expressions which were well calculated to show Colonel Dent where he stood, Grant added a piece of family news:

"I have just received a letter from Fred. He breathes with the most patriotic sentiments. He is for the old flag as long as there is a union of two states fighting under its banner, and when they dissolve he will go it alone. This is not his language but it is the idea not so well expressed as he expresses it. Julia and the children are all well and join me in love to you."

Fred was Frederick T. Dent, Grant's classmate

at West Point. He had gone to the Pacific Coast some years before. The elder Dent was not only a slave owner but he was in sympathy with the southern doctrine, not passively but very aggressively. He had participated in the councils of the secessionists at St. Louis. This letter was dated the 19th of April. It served as an introduction for a visit Grant made to St. Louis a few days later. With W. D. W. Barnard, his wife's relative, Grant went out to the farm and saw Colonel Dent. There was a family council as to where Mrs. Grant and the children had better stay while the husband and father was in the field. It ended in this terse decision by the old fire-eater: "Send Julia and the children here. As you make your bed so you must lie." Colonel Dent lived to see his son-in-law President. He died in the White House.

All that Colonel Dent said has not been quoted in the foregoing. The old slaveholder added: "You were educated in the army, and it's your most natural way to support your family. Go into it and rise as high as you can, but if your troops ever come to this side of the river I will shoot them."

On the tenth of May, 1861, Grant was in St. Louis. He had not then received a commission but was mustering Illinois regiments. One of these regiments was to rendezvous at Belleville. When Grant arrived there only two companies had reported. It was not probable that the others would be in camp for five days. Grant came over to St. Louis. He had not been in the city long until he heard it "whispered that Lyon intended to break up Camp Jackson and capture the militia." He went down to the arsenal to see the troops start for Camp Jackson. Lyon he had known at West Point and also in the army. Blair he had heard speak in the campaign of 1858, but had never met him. As the troops marched out of the arsenal, Blair was on his horse forming them. Grant introduced himself to Blair and had a few moments conversation with him "and expressed my sympathy with his purpose." Until late in the day Grant was a looker on, but before night he became an active participant. In his Memoirs he says:

"Up to this time the enemies of the Government in St. Louis had been bold and defiant, while the Union men were quiet but determined. The enemies had their headquarters in a central and public position on Pine street near Fifth. The Union men had a place of meeting somewhere in the city. I did not know where, and I doubt whether they dared to enrage the enemies of the government by placing the national flag outside of their headquarters. As soon as the news of the capture of Camp Jackson reached the city, the condition of affairs was changed. Union men became rampant, aggressive, and, if you will, intolerant. They proclaimed their sentiments boldly, and were impatient of anything like disrespect for the

Union. The secessionists became quiet but were filled with suppressed rage. They had been playing the bully. The Union men ordered the rebel flag taken down from the building on Pine street. The command was given in tones of authority, and it was taken down never to be raised again in St. Louis.

"I witnessed the scene. I had heard of the surrender of the camp and that the garrison was on its way to the arsenal. I had seen the troops start out in the morning and had wished them success. I now determined to go to the arsenal and await their arrival, and congratulate them. I stepped on a car standing at the corner of Fourth and Pine streets, and saw a crowd of people standing quietly in front of the headquarters, who were there for the purpose of hauling down the flag. There were squads of other people at intervals down the street. They too, were quiet but filled with suppressed rage, and muttered their resentment at the insult to what they called 'their' flag. Before the car I was in had started, a dapper little fellow—he would be called a dude at this day—stepped in. He was in a great state of excitement and used adjectives freely to express his contempt·for the Union and for those who had just perpetrated such an outrage upon the rights of a free people. There was only one other passenger in the car besides myself when this young man entered. He evidently expected to find nothing but sympathy when he got away from the 'mudsills' engaged in compelling a 'free people' to pull down a flag they adored. He turned to me saying: 'Things have come to a — pretty pass when a free people can't choose their own flag. Where I came from if a man dares to say a word for the Union we hang him to a limb of the first tree we come to.' I replied that 'after all we were not so intolerant in St. Louis as we might be; I had not seen a single rebel hung yet, nor heard of one; there were plenty of them who ought to be, however.' The young man subsided. He was so crestfallen that I believe if I had ordered him to leave the car he would have gone quietly out."

Grant went back to Illinois the next day to resume his mustering duties. If he had gone out to Camp Jackson to see the actual capture he would have found Sherman there among the lookers on. John M. Schofield was a major with one of the Union regiments that marched from the arsenal. These three men were to fill the office of lieutenant-general of the regular army. One of the regiments that day was commanded by Colonel Salomon, the man who had defeated Grant for the appointment of superintendent of county roads two years before. Salomon afterwards became colonel of artillery and died of wounds received in battle.

"Colonel Grant moves against Harris" was the headline in a St. Louis paper one July morning in 1861. It gave St. Louisans the first news of "the captain" since his appearance on Fifth street Camp Jackson day. Grant had been made colonel of the Twenty-first Illinois. He marched out of Springfield on the morning of the 3rd of July without waiting for railroad transportation. He was on his way to Northeast Missouri, where bodies of southern sympathizers were stopping railroad traffic and preparing to join Price. Grant moved against Harris. "Tom Harris" he was called. He was a popular leader and had assembled a considerable body of Missourians in camp near the old Missouri town of Florida. A battle between Illinoisans and Missourians was expected by everybody. Grant's orders were to attack. He says:

"As we approached the brow of the hill from which it was expected we could see Harris' camp, and possibly find his men ready formed to meet us, my heart kept getting higher and higher until it felt to me as though it was in my throat. I would have given anything then to have been back in Illinois, but I had not the moral courage to halt and consider what to do; I kept right on. When we reached a point from which the valley below was in full view I halted. The place where Harris had been encamped a few days before was still there and the marks of a recent encampment were plainly visible, but the troops were gone. My heart resumed its place. It occurred to me at once that Harris had been as much afraid of me as I had been of him. This was a view of the

question I had never taken before; but it was one
I never forgot afterwards. From that event to
the close of the war I never experienced trepi-
dation upon confronting an enemy, although I
always felt more or less anxiety. I never forgot
that he had as much reason to fear my forces as I
had his. The lesson was valuable."

Conditions improved rapidly in northeastern
Missouri. Grant made headquarters at Mexico.
Several regiments reported to him although he
was then only a colonel. About the end of July
Grant came back to camp from a short absence
to find the Twenty-first drawn up in line and to
hear a mighty cheer for "General Grant." In
his tent was a telegram from Congressman Washburne addressed to Brigadier-General Grant.
The message read: "You have this day been
appointed brigadier-general of volunteers. Accept
congratulations."

On the 7th of August old acquaintances in St.
Louis were shaking hands with "General Grant."
For several weeks Grant was in and out of St.
Louis, taking orders from Fremont. He wasn't
the same man who had gone away from St. Louis
in the spring of 1860, leaving a number of un-
settled accounts at stores. On one of the earliest
of his official visits to St. Louis, he went from
store to store and paid all of the bills. He knew
just how much was due at each place. He
selected as a staff officer W. C. Hillyer, the young
lawyer of the firm of McClelland, Hillyer and

Moody, where he had occupied deskroom with Boggs. With Hillyer he had discussed politics much during the dull days of 1859. Law business was slow and Hillyer had gone into partnership with William Truesdail, afterwards chief of the secret service with the Army of the Cumberland. They had taken a contract to supply beef to the commissary department, when Hillyer received a telegram from Grant to meet him at the Planter's House. This is what took place:

"Come Hillyer, here's your horse all ready. I have kept a steamer waiting for you three hours. I am going to Cape Girardeau, and want you to go with me on my staff."

"Why, I haven't enlisted."

"No matter for that; you can enlist on the way."

"But I've got no clothes, and no money; my wife expects me home to tea, and my business needs attending to."

"Well, I owe you fifty dollars, and here it is—that will do for money. As for clothes, I guess we have enough among us to supply you. We're ordered to the field and expect a fight with Jeff Thompson. If you survive it I'll give you leave of absence to come home and settle your business."

"But I've just taken a beef contract. I can't keep that and be on your staff."

"That's a fact; so you had better give that up and come along."

Hillyer turned over the contract and went down

the river. The conversation illustrates the change which had come over Grant. On the way to the Cape, Hillyer asked for details. He wanted to know what his rank was to be and whether a commission had been issued to him.

"Well, not exactly," was Grant's reply, "but Fremont, who has authority from the Government promises me he will appoint you. Of course I shall get you the best rank I can. For the present we will call you captain."

Grant was in St. Louis after the capture of Fort Donelson. He came for consultation on the campaign but he took time to call upon old friends. Among these was Henry T. Blow, then a member of Congress. Mr. Blow had been one of Grant's most active supporters when he applied for the position of county superintendent of roads. The conversation naturally turned upon that unsuccessful candidacy. Blow lived in Carondelet. Dr. Taussig's residence was near. Grant said to Blow, who had been much disappointed because the doctor would not vote for the captain: "I wish you would tell Dr. Taussig that I feel much indebted to him for having voted against me when I applied for the position of road superintendent. Had he supported me I might be in that obscure position today instead of being major-general." Mr. Blow called upon Dr. Taussig a few days later and delivered the message.

In his recollections given to the Missouri Historical Society, Dr. Taussig said: "I was driving with John Fenton Long, who was then occupying the position of road superintendent that Grant had applied for, a near neighbor of Dent's and one of the most devoted friends of Grant, under whom he afterwards occupied several high offices, when, at a cross-roads, we met Colonel Dent, and, stopping, engaged in conversation. Long mentioned the famous victory that Grant had accomplished at Fort Donelson, when Dent, interrupting him angrily, said: 'Don't talk to me about this Federal son-in-law of mine. There shall always be a plate on my table for Julia, but none for him.'"

The bark of the father-in-law was a good deal worse than his bite. To be consistent in his position as a southern sympathizer Colonel Dent continued to inveigh against his "Federal son-in-law" but at heart he was proud of Grant from his earliest successes. On the 23rd of January, 1862, Grant was in St. Louis on military business. He rode out to the Gravois farm to see the colonel. The family had not as yet arrived from Galena. Dent received the brigadier with a hearty welcome. Some of the thirty slaves had already taken French leave. It was as Grant had told the colonel, "Slavery is doomed." Dent at once gave orders to one of the faithful servants who remained with him to kill a turkey and get up the best dinner White Haven afforded. Then he sat down for a long talk and made Grant tell him all about the battle of Belmont.

Grant, the General

When Grant began to win victories the lawyers with whom he had his real estate office remembered his inclination to talk about battles. They recalled that they had smiled when Grant read and analyzed the newspaper accounts of the war with which Italy was involved at that time. Grant would discuss the military movements, saying, "This movement was a mistake. If I had commanded the army I would have done thus and so."

Two years later Grant took one of those lawyers to be a member of his staff when he was promoted from colonel to brigadier. He appointed another lawyer from Galena, Rawlins, and a young volunteer officer from the Twenty-first Illinois, his first command. These three civilians thus hurried into the profession of arms, set about learning the science of war as soon as possible. They discussed Jomini. Encountering a proposition which stumped them, they went to Grant for an opinion. The brigadier-general said: "The art of war is simple enough. Find out where your enemy is. Get at him as soon as you can and as often as you can, and keep moving on."

Unexpectedly Major-General Grant arrived in St. Louis on the 26th of January, 1864. The next day a letter, largely signed, was addressed to him. It invited him to a public dinner. The newspaper account said: "If there had been time every citizen of St. Louis would unquestionably have attached his name to the letter." This account is from the Democratic paper. The invi-

76

tation breathed the purpose to show Grant what his fellow citizens of St. Louis felt that they owed him. It said:

"As citizens of Missouri they can never forget the promptness and skill with which you aided in defending the State at the beginning of the conflict when the means at the command of those in authority were wholly inadequate to the great work committed to them."

Grant replied at once to the invitation, explaining the domestic reason for his presence in the city. The fact was that Fred, the oldest son, had been desperately ill with pneumonia when the general was summoned home:

"Your highly complimentary invitation 'to meet old acquaintances and to make new ones' at a dinner to be given by citizens of St. Louis is just received. I will state that I have only visited St. Louis on this occasion to see a sick child. Finding, however, that he has passed the crisis of his disease and is pronounced out of danger by his physician, I accept the invitation. My stay in the city will be short, probably not beyond the 1st proximo. On tomorrow I shall be engaged. Any other day of my stay here, and any place selected by the citizens of St. Louis, will be agreeable for me to meet them."

The dinner was given in the Lindell hotel, which at that time had not been long in operation and which was the pride of the city. A reception in the parlors preceded the dinner. According to the press report Grant "received all with a quiet, modest courtesy characteristic of the man, recognizing old friends and acquaintances with unfailing recollection and friendly greeting." The same report mentions that at the guest tables were two major-generals and seven brigadier-generals. After the three hundred guests had filed into the banquet room, prayer was offered by Rev. Dr. Eliot, the head of Washington University, toward the faculty of which Grant had looked longingly in 1859. Prayer on such an occasion was strictly in accordance with Grant's ideas of propriety. When he led his rather boisterous Twenty-first Illinois into Northwest Missouri, he said to the chaplain of his regiment: "Chaplain, when I was at home and ministers were stopping at my house, I always invited them to ask a blessing at the table. I suppose a blessing is as much needed here as at home, and if it is agreeable with your views, I should be glad to have you ask a blessing every time we sit down to eat."

Judge Samuel Treat presided at the dinner. Grant was introduced as our distinguished guest by Major William W. Dunn. When he arose "a tumultuous shout of welcome went up." This is the newspaper report of the general's speech.

"General Grant: 'In response it will be impossible for me to do more than thank you.' (Enthusiastic applause.)"

The city council voted formally the thanks of the municipality and this, signed by Mayor

Grant, the General

Chauncey I. Filley, was read at the banquet.
Governor Yates, who had given Grant his first
military appointment, sent a telegram: "He is the
hero who never lost a battle." The festivities
lasted until midnight. Orator after orator spoke
of Grant's seventeen victories won up to that
time. Seated among the guests was a grim, old,
white-haired man who had said two years before:
"There shall always be a plate on my table for
Julia, but none for him."

This visit of Grant to St. Louis was of less than
a week. One day the general passed two hours at
the City University where two of his sons were
students under President Edward Wyman. He
went through the institution which then had an
attendance of three hundred. "Yet among all
those youths," wrote the reporter, "not one wore
an air more modest, unpretending and uncon-
scious than that which marked General Grant,
though famed and successful to the highest degree
and charged with the gravest military responsi-
bilities resting upon the shoulders of any general
in the armies of the Union."

Who is this man who has won seventeen victories in the West, who now receives the revived
rank of lieutenant-general, and who comes to
Washington to take command of all of the armies
of the Union? The country was asking in the
winter of 1864. St. Louis papers undertook to
answer. One of them, Democratic, printed what
it claimed was an "authentic biographical sketch"

by "an intimate, personal friend of Lieutenant-General Grant." This intimate personal friend said:

"At the age of twelve he aspired to the management of his father's draught team and was entrusted with it for the purpose of hauling some heavy hewed logs, which were to be loaded with the aid of levers and the usual appliances of several stout men. He came with his team and found the logs but not the men. A boy of more imaginative genius, and of equal but differently directed contrivance, might have laid down to listen or dream, or build houses of chips. Not so this boy, who, unlike others, acted upon the idea that where there was a will there was a way, and hesitated not at the undertaking. Observing a fallen tree having a gradual upward slope, he unhitched his horses, attached them to a log, drew one end of it up the inclined trunk higher than the wagon track and so as to project a few feet over, and thus continued to operate until he had brought several to this position. Next he backed the wagon under the projecting ends, and finally, one by one, hitched to and drew the logs lengthwise across the fallen trunk on to his wagon, hitched up again and returned with his load to his astonished father.

"This anecdote is well remembered by old citizens of Georgetown, Brown county, Ohio, where Grant spent his early boyhood. This incident being similar to many others will not admit of any interpretation other than evidencing an original and uncommon power of adapting measures to conditions. And if, as indeed we think is the plain truth, the true definition of public agent is that he is better than other men only in applying public means to public ends we should not be surprised at the brilliant results of Grant's campaigns, signalized as they are by a boldness, a strategy and comprehensiveness of thought and execution which stamps the character of a great captain. If we never admitted these qualities in the man before, it was because circumstances did not call them into exercise.

"Grant, like his mother before him, never jokes and rarely ever laughs. He never uses a profane or indecent word, abhors dispute, and had never had a personal controversy in his life with boy or man; never made a speech, led a faction, or engaged in idle sport; never sad, he is never gay; always cordial and cheerful, yet always reserved. If he cannot be perfectly sincere, he is perfectly silent. Tolerant, yet enthusiastic, he is always moderate, always earnest. He seems destitute of ostentation, and totally unqualified to display himself even to gratify reasonable curiosity, yet is not ashamed of himself, and appears to contemplate his early and his late career with equal and with simple satisfaction. In a word, there appears nothing of him that is not sterling."

Thus heralded, Grant went East to take command of all of the Union armies.

Grant, the General

In the National Republican convention of 1864 the Missouri delegation voted on the first roll call for Ulysses S. Grant for President. Every other delegation voted for Lincoln. At the close of the roll call, before the announcement of the tellers, the Missouri delegation changed to Lincoln and made his renomination unanimous. Grant had no political aspirations at that time. When one of his friends suggested that his war reputation could be turned to account if he would become a candidate for office, he replied: "I am not a candidate for any office, but I would like to be mayor of Galena long enough to fix the sidewalks, especially the one reaching my house."

Grant did all he could to induce the Missourians not to vote for him in the convention of 1864. He had no thought at that time of ever being a candidate for President. His often avowed ambition was to finish the war and retire to his St. Louis farm. But the instructions of the Missouri state convention to the delegates were to "cast their twenty-two votes for Ulysses S. Grant." After the general had exerted all of his powers of persuasion to prevent the mention of his name in the convention, the Missourians compromised by having their chairman, John F. Hume, cast the vote of the state on the roll call for Grant and then change to Lincoln before the ballot was announced.

Grant's Habits

Grant's Habits

The charge that Grant was a dissipated man got into circulation very early in the war. Before Grant was out of Missouri, in 1861, there occurred a small clash of authority between General Ben M. Prentiss and him. Prentiss thought he was the senior brigadier-general, but the record showed that Grant's commission had been given an earlier date. Fremont placed Grant over Prentiss in the operations of Southeast Missouri. Prentiss came up to St. Louis. Albert D. Richardson, the correspondent of the New York Tribune, met him and expressed surprise to see him in the city. Prentiss replied: "Yes, I have left. I will not serve under a drunkard."

Richardson was with Grant's army much of the time as the campaigning went on down the Mississippi. He summed up his observations on the general's habits:

"On a very few occasions after re-entering the service, the General was perceptibly under the influence of liquor—solely from his extreme susceptibility to it; for ordinarily he did not touch it; and during the entire conflict he probably consumed less than any other officer who tasted it at all. He was never under its sway to the direct or indirect detriment of the service a single moment. And his development was as unique in this as in any other respect. He exhibited the remarkable spectacle of a man in middle life steadily gaining in self control till a propensity once too strong was absolutely mastered."

Grant's Habits

Richardson, in looking up the antecedents of Grant, struck a trail which seemed to lead to inferences which might help to account for the early weakness of liking for whiskey. He visited Georgetown in Brown county, Ohio, where Grant's boyhood was passed. Georgetown is back ten miles from the river. The newspaper correspondent discovered:

"Probably more liquor has been consumed in the vicinity than in any other of our northern communities. To be temperate in Brown means to be intoxicated only two or three times a year. In old times a man who did not get drunk at least on the 8th of January, the 22nd of February, and the 4th of July could hardly maintain his standing in the community or in the local churches."

At the beginning of the war St. Louis supplied the information on which the reports of Grant's dissipation were sent over the country. Newspaper correspondents from other cities found willing talkers on the habits of Grant while he farmed at Hardscrabble. They were given to understand by these gossipers that those habits in respect to drinking were about as bad as they could be. Dr. William Taussig, who saw Grant pass his house coming to and going out from the city, said that Grant's habits at that time were those of "occasional intemperance" and that they "had received much wider notice than there was warrant for."

In his lieutenant days Grant "took his glass of

liquor with the rest of us," was the way a fellow officer put it. At one time, realizing what a hold his liking for whiskey had obtained, Grant joined a temperance organization—the Sons of Temperance. He ceased to be a steady drinker. His intemperance became, as Dr. Taussig described it, occasional. Against the taste Grant struggled, the lapses becoming less and less frequent. A little liquor, which others could take without being affected, showed itself on him. In time Grant conquered and obtained entire control, but through the war and even to the White House he carried the reputation unjustly bestowed upon him in St. Louis.

Henry T. Blow spoke to President Lincoln about the reports that Grant drank whiskey. He was a member of Congress from St. Louis at the time. The newspapers were making much of Grant's habits in the early part of the war. They were charging that the commander was under the influence of liquor most of the time. They were especially sweeping in their criticism immediately after the battle of Shiloh. Blow, who knew the facts, went up to the White House to talk with Mr. Lincoln and to defend Grant if necessary. The President cut short explanations. He said to Blow: "I wish I knew what brand of whiskey he drinks. I would send a barrel to all my other generals."

While Halleck was Grant's superior with headquarters at St. Louis, he took a like humorous view of the stories of Grant's dissipation. The day Halleck received the news of the capture of Donelson he wrote out a brief statement of the victory and put it on the bulletin board in the St. Louis hotel where he was stopping. As an excited crowd gathered to read, Halleck said: "If Grant's a drunkard and can win such victories, I shall issue an order that any man found sober in St. Louis tonight be punished by fine and imprisonment."

These charges of drunkenness were put forward repeatedly during the first two years of the war. As late as the preparations for the battle of Chattanooga, General David Hunter, sent out by Secretary Stanton to inspect and report, felt it proper to include something of Grant's habits:

"I was received by General Grant with the greatest kindness. He gave me his bed, shared with me his room, gave me to ride his favorite horse, read to me his dispatches received and sent, accompanied on my reviews, and I accompanied him on all his excursions. In fact I saw him almost every moment of the three weeks I spent in Chattanooga. He is a hard worker, writes his own dispatches and orders, and does his own thinking. He is modest, quiet, never swears, and seldom drinks, as he only took two drinks while I was with him."

Once a member of the staff wrote about Grant's habits. The letter got into print, to the general's great annoyance. The offense was never repeated.

Grant's Habits

Grant even telegraphed his father that his letters must not be given publicity. The staff officer who offended was Major Webster. He wrote, just after the battle of Shiloh, to Colonel J. S. Stewart:

"I breakfasted with General Grant. I went on board the boat, and rode with him to the field about half past eight in the morning. I was with him all day. I lay down with him on a small parcel of hay which the quartermaster put down to keep us out of the mud, in the rear of the artillery line to the left. He was perfectly sober and self-possessed during the day and the entire battle. No one claimed he was drunk."

Regarding the stories of his drunkenness Grant was "the silent man" so far as voice was concerned. He forbade those nearest to him to make any defense. That he felt the charges keenly the confidential letters he wrote made plain. This is from one in 1862:

"To say that I have not been distressed at these attacks upon me would be false, for I have a father, mother, wife and children who read them and are distressed by them; and I necessarily share with them in it. Then, too, all subject to my orders read these charges and it is calculated to weaken my ability to render efficient service in our present cause. One thing I will assure you of, however—I cannot be driven from rendering the best service within my ability to suppress the present rebellion, and, when it is over, retiring to the same quiet, it, the rebellion, found me enjoying. Notoriety has no charms for me, and could I render the same service that I hope it has been my fortune to render our just cause without being known in the matter, it would be infinitely preferable to me."

Washburne was ever ready to champion Grant. The latter was grateful but he would not consent that even Washburne should come to his defense in this matter of personal character. Grant wrote to Washburne in 1862:

"The great number of attacks made upon me by the press of the country is my apology for not writing to you oftener, not desiring to give any contradiction to them myself. You have interested yourself so much as my friend that should I say anything it would probably be made use of in my behalf."

With his father Grant had more trouble about these charges than with anybody else, to preserve silence. The elder Grant could and did write for the newspapers. In a letter the general took his father to task for something that had been given to a Cincinnati paper and urged him not to do it again:

"You must not expect me to write in my own defense, nor to permit it from anyone about me. I know that the feeling of the troops under my command is favorable to me, and so long as I continue to do my duty faithfully it will remain so. I require no defenders."

Perhaps the only time that Grant opened his

mouth in public upon the subject of his personal habits was when he read his second inaugural address on the 4th of March, 1873:

"Throughout the war and from my candidacy to the present office, in 1868, to the close of the last Presidential campaign, I have been the subject of abuse and slander, scarcely ever equaled in political history, which today I feel that I can afford to disregard, in view of your verdict, which I most gratefully accept as my vindication."

Some one tried to draw out General Sherman in criticism of Grant. The quick-tempered old man broke forth: "It won't do, sir. It won't do. Grant is a great general. He stood by me when I was crazy and I stood by him when he was drunk, and now, sir, we stand by each other." About the same time that the papers were making sweeping charges about Grant's drinking they were asserting that Sherman was insane. Sherman had this in mind when he made use of the language quoted. He wanted to impress upon his listener that the stories of Grant's drunkenness had no more foundation than the allegations against his own sanity.

A recollection of Grant in St. Louis by General Henry Prince illustrated the way in which these stories of intemperance grew. General Prince was at the Planter's when Grant called upon him. The captain was dressed as a farmer, his trousers tucked in his boots, a blacksnake whip in his hands.

Grant's Habits

"I was very glad to see him. I was just coming out of the hotel and met him on the steps going in. I turned to go back with him when he said: 'No, I have only come up to market with a load of wood, and a mutual friend telling me you were here, I have called to ask you to come down to the farm and spend a week with me.' Again I invited him to my apartments in the hotel, but he declined to go, as I supposed then on account of his rough garb. He made no other request of me than to be his guest, and then hastened back to the market place. In this little interview, which began and ended on the steps of the hotel, his manner threw out evidences of his character just as I had always seen and read it in the army and excited my warmest admiration. I have heard a story going the rounds that General Sedgwick had said that I told him, at this interview, Grant was on a spree and had requested the loan of twenty-five cents. I desire to deny in as emphatic terms as I can that such was the fact, and it is utterly impossible that General Sedgwick could have made any such statement. It is purely the creation of some person's idle fancy. I recall the conversation perfectly well in which I related to General Sedgwick this meeting with General Grant in 1859, and of distinctly saying that there was no more appearance of dissipation in Grant's face and manner than in those of a child. I recall how Sedgwick and myself reviewed together the mighty changes four years had brought in Grant. We contrasted the dress in which he had hauled his wood and the uniform of power he was at the moment of our conversation entitled to wear in handling the armies. Both of us agreed that merit, not fortune, was the medium of the phenomenon."

The Clarksville case afforded in the opinion of General James Grant Wilson, one of the best illustrations of the controversy over Grant's habits. As the Union army approached Clarksville early in the war, a committee of safety poured on the ground a large amount of whiskey. The committee did this as a matter of public policy. A report had reached Clarksville, so the committee claimed, that Grant was drunk and unable to control the Union soldiers. Some time afterwards the owners of the whiskey brought suit against the committee of safety for the value of the destroyed liquor. The committee set up the defense indicated. The trial turned on whether Grant was drunk or sober when the Union troops reached Clarksville. On the first trial of the case the jury disagreed, not deciding whether Grant was drunk or sober. On the second trial the verdict found Grant drunk. A third trial was had at which the jury found that the general was perfectly sober. The safety committee lost the case and compromised by paying half of the value of the destroyed whiskey, amounting to some thousands of dollars.

Whatever may have been the measure of truth

about Grant's fondness for whiskey in early years, there is only one side to the testimony on other habits. Grant was clean of speech and person. No one who knew him in the years he lived in St. Louis ever heard him swear. His strongest expletive was "Thunder and Lightning!" And he used that only on great provocation. After he became a farmer he continued to wear his old army overcoat. He wore it so long that on an occasion, seeming to realize that it was becoming rusty, he half apologized with the remark that the garment was made of such good material he didn't like to give it up. There were times when his outer dress was almost shabby. There was no time when he was not fastidious about his underclothing. He said to General Horace Porter: "I have never taken as much satisfaction as some people in making frequent changes of my outer clothing. I like to put on a suit of clothes when I get up in the morning and wear it until I go to bed, unless I have to make a change in my dress to meet company. I have been in the habit of getting one coat at a time, putting it on and wearing it every day as long as it looked respectable, instead of using a best and a second best. I know that it is not the right way to manage, but a comfortable coat seems like an old friend, and I don't like to change it."

Grant was peculiar in respect to diet. He enjoyed his farm living. Corn, beans and many other vegetables he liked. The cucumber was an especial favorite. In the army he was known to make a breakfast on cucumber and coffee. Of meat he ate very little and only that when it was thoroughly cooked. A rare steak was an abomination to him. He cared nothing for game and did not hunt. Poultry he would not touch. He had a saying that he "never could eat anything that goes on two legs." As a result of this taste, Grant let many courses at public dinners pass untouched. He was considered a very small eater. Of fruit he was fond and ate it slowly, as if to prolong the enjoyment.

No intoxicating liquor was served at Grant's table in private or public life, in peace or in war, save only at formal state dinners in the White House. During the war, the general would sometimes join the members of his staff in a drink of whiskey and water at the end of a long ride in bad weather, but he never had anything but coffee, tea and water on the mess table and never offered liquor to visitors.

Grant, the President

Grant, the President

While he was in the White House Grant came to the rescue of St. Louis. It was at a time when high officials and old friends were conspiring to disgrace his administration through internal revenue frauds. Grant was an admirer of James B. Eads. The great engineer's steady persistence and masterly ability in overcoming obstacles and accomplishing his ends appealed strongly to the man who had shown the same qualities in the war. Friendship between Grant and Eads dated back to the building of the iron clad gunboats by Eads. These boats were turned out in such time as seemed almost incredible when the contracts were given. They counted for much in Grant's plans to open the Mississippi and thus split the Confederacy in two. Eads was building the St. Louis bridge which bears his name while Grant was President. He had put into it the profits of the gunboat contracts and had about exhausted the local capital support. Engineering and financial problems were not all that made the work difficult. Steamboat interests were unfriendly. They had opposed any bridging of the Mississippi. In 1873 the Keokuk Packet line filed a complaint with the Secretary of War that the Eads bridge was an obstruction to commerce. The complaint set forth that, in high water, boats could not pass under the arches without lowering their smokestacks. The steamboat people asked the government to remove the bridge. At that time work on the upper structure was nearing completion.

Grant, the President

The opening of the bridge for traffic was promised for the following year. Judge Taft of Cincinnati, father of former President Taft, had been Secretary of War while the earlier construction of the bridge was going on. The complaint of the steamboat people had not been made to him. The Keokuk Packet line managers saw an opportunity when Belknap succeeded Judge Taft. Belknap was a Keokuk man. He later retired from the cabinet upon the exposure of the post tradership scandals involving a member of his family. Belknap entertained the complaint of his steamboat friends. He appointed a commission which confined its investigation mainly to the testimony of the steamboat men. General John W. Noble, their attorney, attempted in vain to get a hearing for the bridge people.

St. Louis had watched the building of the bridge day by day for five years. The city saw a great trade territory to the northwest slipping away because the river had been bridged above while at her front it ran unfettered to the sea, the barrier to east and west commerce. A great shock came to St. Louisans when the report of Belknap's commission was made public. The commission found that while the bridge had been built in exact accordance with the Act of Congress it was nevertheless an obstruction to navigation. The report recommended that the bridge should come down or that a ship canal be dug around the east end of it, advising that the subject be brought to the attention of Congress. The bridge company at that time had expended $6,000,000, practically exhausting its resources. Negotiations for the money necessary to complete the bridge were in progress. They were threatened with failure if Belknap's commission report went to Congress. Dr. William Taussig, in his recollections preserved by the Missouri Historical Society, tells how Grant came to the rescue:

"In this emergency Captain Eads and I concluded to appeal to the President, and on a hot July morning we appeared at the White House, sent in our cards and were promptly admitted. Upon our entering the cabinet, President Grant met Captain Eads with outstretched hands, greeting warmly, and then, turning toward me, said, with a facetious smile, while shaking hands with me: 'How are you, Judge?' I noticed the allusion at once and said: 'Mr. President, by addressing me as 'Judge' I hope you do not recall a former event which has weighed heavily on my mind ever since you have attained your high position.' He laughed and said: 'Oh, no; you see how much better it is than it might have been.'

"We stated our case and he listened seriously and attentively. He had never heard of this commission—its appointment or action. After awhile he rang the bell and sent for the Secretary. General Belknap soon entered, and the President at once, rapidly and curtly, asked him a few categorical questions—had the bridge been built in accordance with the provisions of the Act of Congress, and had the structure been approved by the former Secretary of War? Belknap said yes, but claimed the general authority under the law given to the Secretary of War to remove obstructions to navigation, and offered to send for all the papers in the case.

"The President said nothing for awhile, and then, with that peculiar firm set of his lower jaw, substantially said: 'I do not care to look at the papers. You certainly cannot remove this structure on your own judgment. If Congress were to order its removal it would have to pay for it. It would hardly do that in order to save high smoke-stacks from being lowered when passing under the bridge. If your Keokuk friends feel aggrieved let them sue the bridge people for damages. I think, General, you had better drop the case.'

"Belknap, whose face had colored a deep red, rose and, with a bow, left the cabinet. We left soon, with warm thanks, and were enabled to inform the public and our bankers that this vexatious proceeding had been entirely abandoned by order of the President.

"I remember particularly one raw, cold November day in 1873, when he came to our office, accompanied by the late Captain Couzins and Mr. Chauncey I. Filley, and went out with Captain Eads and Colonel Henry Flad, the assistant chief engineer, to walk over the first two arches, over which only a few narrow planks had been laid.

It was hard and risky work, even for those accustomed to it. But, as Colonel Flad told me, the President walked over it fearlessly and took in everything that was shown him with much interest. Upon the return of the party Captain Eads took a bottle of brandy out of his closet, I brought out my box of cigars, and we all sat down around a draughtsman's deal table. The President and those with him were nearly frozen and he and they enjoyed the brandy. He smoked cigars rapidly and had them half chewed up when he threw them away. His conversation and demeanor were as quiet, modest and unassuming as those of any private citizen. While looking at him I had always to recall to my mind and to realize that it was not an ordinary citizen who sat and chatted at this table, but the greatest man of his time.

"History has already inscribed this great character, and what the country owes to him, upon its tablets, but only a few have been privileged to know his plain, unassuming disposition, the ease with which he turned from the lofty eminence of the Presidential chair into the position of a plain citizen, the loyalty with which he clung, often to his own discomfort and disparagement, to old friends and adherents, and withal the quiet, impressive dignity which distinguished this unpretending democratic citizen President."

St. Louis men and women in numbers, who had known Grant in the Gravois days, were welcomed warmly at the White House. As he drove his wood wagon to and from the city, Grant had often stopped at the home of the Masure family on Chouteau avenue. Mrs. Masure had been Miss Amanda Chenie. Following the hospitable traditions of old St. Louis, Mrs. Masure had, as often as he called, insisted that "the captain" remain for dinner. After he became President, one of the first appointments made by Grant was that conferred upon a son of Mrs. Masure. Later Mrs. Masure was a guest at the White House and was introduced by the President personally as "an old and valued friend." But Grant's remembrance of the hospitality was shown in a way even more practical and suggestive of his entertainment in the former days at the Masure home. When Mrs. Masure left Washington to return to St. Louis, there was delivered to her on the train, with a personal message from the President, a basket containing the best lunch which the White House chef could prepare.

President Grant looked back upon the wood hauling period with no sense of humiliation or bitterness. He recalled it as an interesting experience with some humorous episodes. When he was about to enter upon his first term as President, he, with Mrs. Grant, was entertained by Mr. and Mrs. Henry T. Blow. At that time, in 1868-9, the home of the Blows was one of the most beautiful suburban places of St. Louis. It was in Carondelet, which Mr. Blow hoped to see become "the Birmingham of America." The Blows were hospitable people, entertaining with the charm of St. Louis custom. Old friends were invited to meet General and Mrs. Grant. The gathering was in the nature of a farewell to White Haven and godspeed to the White House. After dinner Grant suggested a walk through the grounds. As he led the way he showed keen interest in recognizing the familiar surroundings. He pointed where he had driven in the backyard his team to deliver wood from the Gravois farm. But what the general dwelt upon was the location of a certain tree. He said that on one of his trips, bringing the cordwood, he had, with possible carelessness, let a hub of the wagon strike that tree and bark it badly. The tree was a favorite of Mrs. Blow's, one which she had watched develop and of which she was proud. Before Grant could unload and get away, Mrs. Blow came out and saw the damage. Grant smiled broadly as he told the party of guests that Mrs. Blow "gave me such a scoring as I never before or since have received from a woman." One of the guests present, who heard the general tell the story was the late Judge Charles W. Irwin of Kirkwood, who repeated it, shortly after the dinner, to his friend and neighbor, Judge Enos Clarke.

brought out. Let no guilty man escape if it can be avoided. Be specially vigilant — or instruct those engaged in the prosecution of frauds to be — against all who insinuate that they have high influence to protect, or to protect them. No personal consideration should stand in the way of performing a public duty.

U. S. Grant

July 29th /75

Referred to the Sec. of the Treas. This was intended as a private letter for my information, and contained many extracts from St. Louis papers not deemed necessary to forward. They are obtainable and have no doubt been all read by the federal officials in St. Louis. I forward this for information in to the end that if it throws any light upon new parties to summons as witnesses they may

Grant and the Whiskey Ring

Grant and the Whiskey Ring

Three St. Louis men wrote books on Grant. One of these books was published in 1887. It took up Grant's battles, one after the other, and showed that his military career was a succession of blunders. It convicted the general of utter ignorance of the science of war. Another of these books appeared in 1879. It was called the "Great American Empire." Grant was exposed as a man of despotic, vindictive nature, bent upon making himself dictator of the United States. If Grant succeeded in becoming Emperor of North America, Roscoe Conkling was to be the Duke of New York. The third book was published in 1880, after the defeat of the third term movement. It purported to be "a complete exposure of the illicit whiskey frauds culminating in 1875." It alleged that Grant was "an active participant in the frauds." These St. Louis authors did not regard themselves as humorists. The author, or putative author, of the "Secrets of the Great Whiskey Ring," was John McDonald, the head of the conspiracy. At the close of his three hundred and more pages of "evidence" McDonald, in summing up his revelations, disclaimed knowledge that any part of the $2,786,000 revenue, of which he said the government was robbed in his district, went directly to Grant. What he claimed was that "Grant knew" money was raised by these frauds to finance political campaigns of which he was the beneficiary.

President Grant arrived in St. Louis from

Washington the evening of the 5th of October, 1874. He was accompanied by Mrs. Grant and their daughter, Secretary of the Navy Borie and General Babcock. Ten old friends and Federal officials were at the station to meet and welcome the Presidential party. Within the following year four of the ten were convicted of complicity in the Whiskey Ring and were in prison.

The President had come to visit "the Grant farm." He had timed his visit so that he could be present at the St. Louis Fair. Both while he was lieutenant-general and President, Grant received many gifts of livestock. His admirers bestowed upon him colts, calves and pigs with pedigrees, but especially colts. Grant permitted the manager of the farm to show some of his livestock at the Fair. The management of the Fair encouraged the entries by Grant as attractions of popular interest. As regularly as he could make it convenient the general came to St. Louis in Fair time. One year an enormous steer from the Grant farm was exhibited for the benefit of the Soldiers' Orphan Home at Webster Groves, the President consenting to it at the request of the managers of the institution. The steer weighed about two thousand pounds. It was driven from the farm on the Gravois road to the Fair Grounds with much difficulty. Admission to the tent was charged, the money being given to the asylum. The steer stood the week of the Fair, but on the way back to the farm it lay down and died.

Grant and the Whiskey Ring

In connection with Grant's visit to the Fair in 1874 occurred an unpleasant incident. It was only a day's local sensation at the time, but before twelve months had rolled around it had been magnified into national concern. It became an important part of the circumstantial evidence by which conspirators sought to implicate Grant in the Whiskey Ring.

The President visited the Fair on the 6th of October. He requested that his presence be not announced or noticed with any formality. A seat was given him on the platform under the pagoda in the center of the amphitheater. There he sat, smoking the inevitable cigar, chatting occasionally with Secretary Borie and looking at the entries being judged. That day Grant had two entries, Claymore and Young Hambletonian. This is Charles G. Gonter's account of the incident of which so much was subsequently made by the head of the Whiskey Ring:

"A ring of thoroughbreds was being judged. The twelve or fifteen exhibits included some of the best products of the stock farms of Kentucky. In those days the St. Louis Fair was the annual event of the kind for the Mississippi Valley. One of the youngsters was entered in the name of General Grant. The colt had been given, perhaps, from motives of friendship, possibly on account of politics. He was a fairly good animal but was outclassed. That could be seen at a glance by any one with knowledge of horses.

Grant and the Whiskey Ring

The general was standing near me. He turned and said, 'Charley, what do you think of them?'

"We had been acquainted many years. I had known him when he was Captain Grant in St. Louis before the war. He always called me 'Charley.' I knew the general's entry was in that ring and I knew the general knew it. I gave him a perfectly frank answer as he expected, pointing out one of the Kentucky-bred horses that in my judgment was entitled to the blue ribbon. The general confirmed my opinion without any hesitation, saying: 'I guess you are right.'

"Well, the judges went around the ring several times looking over the entries and having them galloped to and fro. They seemed to be having trouble about the decision. After a long while it was announced that the judges couldn't agree; that they were evenly divided. The rule was, in such cases, to call in an outsider to give the casting vote. General John McDonald was named. The decision came quickly. The judges stepped up to the President's colt and tied on the blue ribbon. General Grant was close by me. As I looked at him, he flushed, took his cigar out of his mouth, threw it on the ground and said in a low voice: 'That is an outrage.'

"He turned and walked away. The award was so clearly unfair that everybody was talking about it. Soon the directors of the Fair went to their rooms to lunch together. As was the custom the amphitheater reporters accompanied them. After the lunch the president of the Fair Association said to the reporters: 'You gentlemen of the press know what was done in the judging of that last ring of colts. For the Fair directors I can say that we had rather have had a rainy day spoiling the attendance than to have seen such an act of injustice in our amphitheater. We leave the matter in your hands to treat as you see fit.'

"The newspaper men conferred but didn't decide upon anything. I went ahead on my own hook, wrote a full story of just what had happened. The *Globe* printed what I wrote. Early in the morning, before I started for the Fair Grounds, I received a call to come to the office of William McKee, the senior proprietor of the paper. As I went in he said: 'Charley, you've ruined us.'

" 'What is the matter?' I asked him.

" 'Why, that report of the award to General Grant's horse,' he said.

" 'I wrote just what happened,' said I. 'Everybody who was there will tell you so.'

" 'I know,' said Mr. McKee, 'but it will hurt us over in Illinois. We will lose our subscribers. They worship Grant over there and they will think this is an attack on him.'

" 'Who says so?' I asked.

" 'Johnny McDonald,' said Mr. McKee, 'he was in here a little while ago.'

" 'Well,' said I, 'when I went out to report the amphitheater you gave me a sheet of white paper and told me to report just what happened without favor to anybody and I've followed the instructions the best I knew how.'

"I left the office and went to the Fair Grounds expecting to be relieved at any hour. Along in the afternoon Mr. McKee came out. When he saw me, he walked over and said: 'Charley, that article about the award to Grant's horse was all right.'

" 'Who says so?' I asked.

" 'The general himself,' Mr. McKee replied. 'He was in the office awhile after you left, said you had made a correct report of what occurred and he thanked us for printing it.' "

Gonter's report of the incident, for printing which President Grant thanked the *Globe*, was as follows:

"We had in this ring one of the finest collections that has appeared in the arena for many years, representing some of the best roadster blood extant—Golddust, Daniel Boone, Green Mountain, Black Hawk, Morgan, Highlander, Hamilton, Ewald's Dixie, Nig Peacemaker, and Alexander's Abdallah. Better could not have been collected within the arena of an amphitheater. The horses were all speeded and some of them showed excellent trotting qualities. After considerable delay, the judges tied the blue ribbon upon the head of President Grant's Claymore, by Peacemaker. It is seldom we take exception to the action of committees, but in this instance we feel compelled to dissent. In our opinion as well as in the opinion of nearly every judge of this noble animal upon the ground yesterday, this award was regarded with amazement and astonishment, in such a collection, embracing as it did, the very best horses in the country. In all due deference it seemed to us that the ribbon was given as a compliment to the President and not to the animal."

In the book which he published six years after the St. Louis Fair incident McDonald gave his version of the award to Grant's horse. He coupled with that incident his story of the gift of a team to the President. In a conversation at Washington, McDonald said, Grant had complained that his stock did not receive premiums at the Fair. He urged the President to make an exhibition in 1874. On his return to St. Louis he called upon the president of the Fair and repeated the complaints of General Grant:

"Mr. Barret replied that the reason President Grant had not been given a premium was because his stock had been entered in competition with that which was superior, and the committees did not wish to show partiality to any one. After talking with him a while he told me that I might be placed on the committee that would award the premiums on stock, and, if I wished to assume the responsibility, the President's stock might secure a premium."

McDonald says he took the position and when the President's entry was brought in the ring he told a member of the committee there was one thing he wanted done; obtaining consent to which, he would favor anything they wished:

"This one thing was to give the first premium to the President's stallion, and, although there were several preeminently superior horses in competition, the other members of the committee endorsed my act and awarded the blue ribbon.

"At the time I had a pair of fast horses and tendered them to President Grant while he remained in the city. I was with Grant on several occasions while he was in St. Louis, and he was greatly pleased with the team. Being a subordinate officer and wishing to ingratiate myself into the good graces of His Excellency, and knowing his weakness for fine horseflesh, I told him I would present him with the team, but in such a way that it would appear as if he had purchased them. I had the bills for the wagon, harness and equipments made out in the name of the President and had the team taken to Washington by Nat Carlin, the superintendent of the President's farm. The first week in December, 1874, I dropped in at the White House the very day Congress assembled, and saw the President in his office. He had used the team for some time and was delighted with them. I told him that I had a bill of sale made out, with minor bills attached, amounting in all to about $1,750, if my memory serves me rightly. The bill was receipted and signed before I started from St. Louis. I asked him with a smile to hand me a few dollars. He pulled out a fifty dollar bill, and threw it at me, and asked if that would do. I told him it was too much and threw it back. Then the President gave me a ten dollar bill, and I took out of my vest pocket a five dollar bill and a two dollar bill, which I gave to him in change, thus leaving me three dollars for the team."

Before the war McDonald was a "steamboat runner" on the St. Louis levee. That is to say, he exerted himself in a variety of energetic ways to secure passengers for the line he represented. He was a small, wiry man with much nerve and no education. After his marriage Mrs. McDonald taught him to read and write. When hostilities began, McDonald's acquaintance with river men, together with his faculty of leadership enabled him to get recruits. He did so much toward the organization of the Eighth Missouri that he was given a commission. He rose to be major of the regiment which distinguished itself for hard fighting under Sherman. At the close of the war, McDonald was breveted brigadier-general. For several years his business was pushing claims against the quartermaster department at Washington. He made considerable money out of commissions on what he collected.

In 1868, Congress created supervisors of internal revenue in order to lessen frauds against the government. Supervisors were put in charge of districts to check up the work of collectors. McDonald applied for a supervisorship. He filed remarkable indorsements from St. Louis. General Sherman, James E. Yeatman who had been foremost in the relief work for wounded soldiers and who was known nationally as "Old Sanitary," Mayor Nathan Cole, Judges Irwin Z. Smith and James S. Farrar, Ex-Governor Thomas C. Fletcher, James B. Eads, President George P. Plant of the Merchants' Exchange, Lieutenant-Governor E. O. Stanard, and others who were among the best known and most highly esteemed citizens of St. Louis gave endorsements. Some of the letters spoke of McDonald's energy and loyalty. Some of them expressed the opinion that he would discharge the duties faithfully and honestly. There had been revenue frauds in the preceding administration under Andrew Johnson. It was to put a stop to abuses that supervisors were created. Senator Carl Schurz, Congressman D. P. Dyer, District Attorney John W. Noble, United States Marshal Newcomb, and Congressman G. A. Finkelnburg united in a protest against the appointment of McDonald. They said in their telegram to Secretary Boutwell:

"We beg leave to assure you that the reputation of this man and his associates are such that can bring no moral support to the government in the enforcement of the internal revenue laws, and that it is quite certain that his qualifications, natural or acquired, are such as to render the appointment an unfit one to be made."

McDonald was appointed in November, 1869,

his district at first being Arkansas and the Indian Territory. Three months later Missouri was added and St. Louis became the headquarters. That same year the Liberal Republican movement, on a platform of enfranchisement of Confederates, swept Missouri, the Democrats making no nominations. B. Gratz Brown was elected governor. Inspired by their success, the Liberal Republicans in Missouri began to organize for a national campaign in 1872, with the view of defeating Grant for re-election, his nomination by the regular Republican party being assured. McDonald, being the chief Federal official in St. Louis, became prominent with the regular Republicans. He was very active openly. Secretly he organized the Whiskey Ring which went into operation September, 1871. The avowed object of the ring among the members of it was to raise money for Grant's re-election. Conduce G. Megrue, who had been president of a national bank in Ohio, was brought to St. Louis and given charge of details. Ostensibly his business here was the agency of a patent paving company. Until the Presidential election of 1872, the ring operated and considerable sums were turned over to national campaign managers. The money came freely from McDonald and others. No questions were asked. As much as $30,000, it was said, was sent to Indiana for the October election.

The ring's plan of operations was simple.

Government officials allowed distillers to run a specified percentage of their output untaxed. Of the untaxed product the distillers paid the ring one-half of the amount which would have gone to the government if the tax had been paid. The magnitude of the St. Louis frauds may be realized when it is stated that the conspirators received during considerable periods $8,500 a week. During the last year of the ring's operations it was said that the government's loss at St. Louis was $1,500,000. To carry on the frauds required complicity of storekeepers and gaugers. These men were corrupted.

The frauds were conducted so successfully before the election of 1872 that in 1873 the ring was reorganized and resumed operations. Now, there was no pretence of party necessity. The money was distributed regularly in St. Louis. Occasional remittances were made to Washington officials. Gaugers and storekeepers and other subordinates were carried on the ring payroll at from $50 to $100 a month. The greater part of the fund was divided into five parts, one of which was mysteriously set apart for "the man in the country." Each of the ringleaders netted $1,000 and upwards a week.

The frauds were apparent. The existence of the ring was known to many. Comparison of the shipments of high wines by rail from St. Louis with the number of gallons paying tax for a given period showed the illicit distilling. The figures

were of record. Treasury agents came out inter-
mittently with orders to investigate. Advance
information of the coming was sent to the St.
Louis managers by Washington segments of the
ring. Sometimes packages of $5,000 or $10,000
were placed in the hands of these agents or thrown
over the transoms into their hotel rooms. The
agents reported they could find nothing wrong.
"Put your house in order" telegraphed from
Washington meant the coming of agents who
could not be corrupted. Then distillers were told
to run straight until further notice.

One vital element of strength held the ring together. That was the oft-repeated assertion "the
old man knows." There was a single connection
between the ring and "the old man." That link
was McDonald. The supervisor maintained such
relations with the President that he convinced his
co-conspirators, the official rank and file and the
distillers they were safe. The supervisor achieved
this generally through his political activity in behalf of the administration but specifically through
his adroit catering to the President's fondness for
horses.

What seemed to be the crucial test of McDonald's relationship with the President came when a
general order was issued by direction of Secretary
Bristow shifting the supervisors. McDonald was
ordered to go to Philadelphia. That meant the
death knell of the St. Louis Whiskey Ring.
McDonald went to Washington and saw the

President. The order was revoked by direction
of Grant. McDonald came back to St. Louis vic-
torious. The conspirators believed more strongly
than ever before that "the old man knew."
Nevertheless the lightning struck. The ring was
shattered. Grant wrote his historic endorsement
on the St. Louis revelations: "Let no guilty man
escape." Month after month McDonald told his
fellow conspirators "the old man" didn't mean
it. He was indicted, tried and convicted. He
said he would be pardoned immediately. He
wore stripes seventeen months in the Missouri
penitentiary. Other ringleaders suffered with
their chief. Minor officials and distillers were
indicted but let off with mild punishment on
pleas of guilty, in consideration of their testimony
given against the leaders. Only one indicted man
escaped. He was General Babcock. A grand
jury headed by one of the men who had indorsed
McDonald for supervisor indicted Babcock.
A jury acquitted on the strength of Grant's
testimony.

A former United States Senator from Missouri,
John B. Henderson, was chosen by the Attorney-
General to aid the district attorney, D. P. Dyer,
in the prosecution of the Whiskey Ring. In one
of the earlier trials, General Henderson, referring
to the interference with the commissioner of
internal revenue, said:

"What right had Babcock to go to Douglass and
induce him to withdraw his agents. Douglass

was placed in his position to see that the revenue laws of the government were properly enforced. What business then had Douglass with him? When an official goes into office, he should be free and independent of all influences except that of law, and if he recognizes any other master, then this government is tumbling down. What right had the President to interfere with Commissioner Douglass in the proper discharge of his duties or with the Secretary of the Treasury? None. And Douglass showed a lamentable weakness of character when he listened to Babcock's dictates. He should either have insisted that his orders, as they existed, be carried out, or should have resigned his office. Now, why did Douglass bend the supple hinges of his knee and permit any interference by the President? This was Douglass' own business, and he stood responsible for it under his official oath. He was bound to listen to no dictation from the President, Babcock, or any other officer and it was his duty to see that that order was carried out, or resign. Would that we had officials who possessed more of that sterner stuff of which the office-holders of olden times were made! Why do they not leave their office when they cannot remain there honorably? Is it to be that because a man holds an office at the hands of another, he is to be a bonded slave?"

When the news of General Henderson's speech reached Washington, the attorney-general telegraphed for the official stenographic report of that part relating to the President's interference with the commissioner of internal revenue in respect to the order moving the supervisors. A cabinet meeting was called. "I am not on trial," Grant was reported to have said. Henderson was removed and in his place as special prosecutor James O. Broadhead was appointed. This action was widely interpreted as evidence of the President's interest in the indicted and of a purpose to defeat the ends of justice. It gave hope to those whose trials were approaching. As the time for the trial of his secretary, General Babcock, drew near, the President did another thing, extraordinary and without precedent in the history of the country. He prepared to come to St. Louis to testify for the defense. After the trial began, the presence of the President was waived and by agreement between the prosecution and the defense his deposition was taken at the White House before the Chief Justice of the United States Supreme Court. President Grant testified that he at first approved the order transferring supervisors and then revoked it. He explained his change of mind:

"Sometime when Mr. Richardson was Secretary, I think at all events before Secretary Bristow became the head of the department, Mr. Douglass in talking with me expressed the idea that it would be a good plan occasionally to shift the various supervisors from one district to another. I expressed myself favorably towards it, but it was not done then; nor was it thought of any more by me until it became evident that the Treasury was being defrauded of a portion of the revenue it should receive from the distillation of spirits in the West. Secretary Bristow at that time called upon me and made a general statement of his suspicions, when I suggested to him this idea. On that suggestion the order making these transfers of supervisors was made. At that time I did not understand that there was any suspicion at all of the officials, but that each official had his own way of transacting his business. These distillers, having so much pecuniary interest in deceiving the officials, learn their ways and know how to avoid them. My idea was that by putting in new supervisors, acquainted with their duties, over them, they would run across and detect their crooked ways."

The order of transfer was issued. President Grant told why he revoked the order:

"I resisted all efforts to have the order revoked until I became convinced that it should be revoked or suspended in the interest of detecting frauds that had already been committed. In my conversation with Supervisor Tutton, he said to me that if the object of that order was to detect frauds that had already been committed, he thought it would not be accomplished. He remarked that this order was to go into effect on the 15th of February. This conversation took place late in January. He alleged that it would give the distillers who had been defrauding the Treasury three weeks notice to get their houses in order, and be prepared to receive the new supervisor; that he, himself, would probably go into a district where frauds had been committed and he would find everything in good order, and he would be compelled to so report; that the order would probably result in stopping the frauds at least for a time, but would not lead to the detection of those that had already been committed. He said that if the order was revoked, it would be regarded as a triumph for those that had been defrauding the Treasury. It would throw them off their guard, and he could send special agents of the Treasury to the suspected distillers—send good men, such a one as he mentioned, Mr. Brooks. They could go out and would not be known to the distillers, and before they could be aware of it, the latters' frauds could be detected; the proofs would be complete, the distilleries could be seized, and their owners prosecuted. I felt so conscious that his argument was sound, and that it was in the interest of the detection and punishment of fraud that this order should be suspended, I then told him that I would suspend it immediately, and I did so without further consultation with anyone. My recollection is that I wrote the direction for the suspension of the order on a card, in pencil, before leaving my office that afternoon, and that the order was issued and sent to the Treasury by one of my secretaries."

Grant and the Whiskey Ring

In his deposition the President reiterated in various forms that Secretary Babcock had never by word or act sought to influence him in behalf of the Whiskey Ring. Two questions and answers, one on direct, the other on cross-examination, will serve to illustrate the whole deposition.

"Q. 'Have you ever seen anything in the conduct of General Babcock, or has he ever said anything to you which indicated to your mind that he was in any way interested in or connected with the Whiskey Ring at St. Louis or elsewhere?' A. 'Never.'

"Q. 'Perhaps you are aware, General, that the Whiskey Ring have persistently tried to fix the origin of that ring in the necessity for funds to carry on the political campaign; did you ever have any intimation from General Babcock or any one else, in any manner, directly or indirectly, that any funds for political purposes were being raised by any improper methods?' A. 'I never did. I have seen since these trials intimations of that sort in the newspapers, but never before.'"

McDonald incorporated in his book some letters and telegrams which were not produced in the series of trials but not one of these proved that Grant knew. In the course of the trials, counsel for the defense intimated that the prosecution was smirching the President. General Henderson replied:

"It is my sacred opinion that the President knew

127

nothing of these frauds. I protest solemnly against such declarations as that just made. It is my solemn opinion that the President has been grossly deceived by his professed friends here and in Washington and that he neither knew nor suspected the depth of rascality going on here."

The grand jury which found the indictment against Babcock adopted a resolution vindicating and commending the President. Lawyers for the prosecution, newspaper men who worked for months on the Whiskey Ring revelations, grand jurymen who sought the uttermost ends of the conspiracy—all have gone on record that nowhere did evidence appear that Grant had guilty knowledge of the ring, much less that he had any share in the spoils. Only one man has asserted that "Grant knew." That man was McDonald. Upon his word rests the case. The "Secrets of the Great Whiskey Ring" were told adroitly. The telegrams and letters of the conspirators were massed with skill. They were circumstantial but not conclusive without McDonald's inferences and assertions.

To Andrew D. White, Grant put forth this challenge: "If you find me guilty of any share in a dishonest act drag me forth and expose me."

When Secretary Bristow was unwilling to answer certain questions asked about the Whiskey Ring by Congress, Grant sent this message to him: "I beg to relieve you from all obligations of secrecy on this subject and desire not only that you may answer all questions relating to it but that all members of my cabinet may also be called upon to testify in the same matter."

In the Bixby collection of Grant letters is the historic indorsement "Let no guilty man escape." It was written by President Grant on the back of a long letter from W. D. W. Barnard who marked it "Confidential." The wife of Barnard was a relative of Mrs. Grant. At that time the grand jury was investigating the Whiskey Ring and had returned some indictments. Babcock had not been indicted, but was referred to in the letter.

Confidential   Kirkwood, Mo., July 19th, 1875.
Dear General:

Writing Genl Sherman in my behalf in 1864, you done me the high honor to close with,

"Mr. Barnard, has been a sincere friend of mine, when I wanted friends and when there was no apparent possible chance of him ever deriving any benefit from it, you may trust Mr. B. with the assurance that he will betray no trust."

Valueing these assurances of your high regard and confidence.—I need hardly tell you how assiduously I have striven to prove worthy of, and maintain same—Or refer to history for the re-occuring evidence of the many-fold intricaces of polished inuendo and intrigue, indulged in, around Power—instigated by Place, Jelousy, Unfriendliness, Revenge, &c, &c—From evidence in my possession, I feel that I have not escaped the efforts of such; to place us in antagonism. But I am rewarded by the consciousness of your generous feelings of old.

If, there ever was a time, when, your true admirers should exert themselves, in this section, to correct the inferences, sought to be created, against you, by your political adversaries and unworthy parties here, who have occupied place and dastardly outraged confidence—with others yet in office—It has been, the past three months.

The "clips" enclosed, from the *Republican* and *Times* of today—marked "A" and "B"—show some of the many efforts, to tarnish your great name—by implication—that from the *Republican*, it is intimated, bears the "ear marks" of John B. Henderson—assisting in the prosecution of cases before the Grand Jury—the closing of which is simply infamous—and I fear, aided in his old animosity, by a report whispered around, since Casey left the city, by the apologists of the "ring," that he said, "Mr. Bristow had deceived you and would not retain the Tres'y portfolio thirty days"—I have denied this assertion, when made in my presence and have written him what has been said.

Neither Henderson and Dyer like a bone in your body—they will do what generality of lawyers consider their duty—nothing more—and both inspired with political aspirations, will take good care to advance what they may regard their own, or friends interest.

Grant and the Whiskey Ring

Feeling thus, I can not but think, that the interest of the Government and your own past record, should be protected by additional counsel—known to be actuated by the highest sense of duty and fielty—regardless of the prospective influence of press—Party—or self angrandisement— * * * * is a mere stick and had it not been for high family and social influences, it is pretty well understood, would have been impeached in his * * * office sometime since.

Again, as I have had occasion to say to Mr. Newcomb himself, I do not believe there will be a conviction of the indited, whilst he retains the Marshalship—convinced of this, of what I know has occured and occuring, I can not but state it to you—the reasons for which would make this communication too lengthy although I premise, who the secreted hand is, that holds him in power—and why.

*** ** ***, it has been generally understood for years, has been head and ears cognisant of—an abettor—and participant of the "ring swag"—as far back as 71, it is stated and believed that he asserted your being consulted and consenting to the ring—received two portions of the divide—with the understanding among the initiated, that one part was for the lamented Ford—not one cent of which I am confident was ever proffered—did he get—or would have taken.

I am creditably informed that these facts could have been brought out, but for interviews

131

with and influences brought to bear upon a wit-
ness and a seeming studdied effort to shield him
*** under the audacious assertion that his inditement, would lead to exposures that would strike so
high, as to distroy the Party of the Republic.

*** should be called before the Grand Jury and
probed to the quick—but parties herein named,
with Benton, Blow, Walsh (endorsers on Democrat purchase), Maguire, Newcomb and others,
do not want it—an inditement could and should
be had, but may not take place, from influences
exerted and will be continued, to save him—and
in after time, will be said, would have been, but
for protecting others—and this by some of the
very men herein named.

Col. Normeile prosecuting Circuit Atty—
McDonald and Joyce's confidential friend, asked
me Saturday "how far matters were going to be
pushed towards them"—said, I thought until the
last man made restitution to his utmost ability to
pay and were punished to the extent of the law—
if local officers done their duty. He replied that
both had told him, that day when seeking bail—
"that you could not give them up, or Babcock
would be lost"—(this is the kind of talk indulged
in and frequently by the "*** claquers" speaking
as openly of you) I said, they, or anyone, who
talks that way, little knew the stuff of which you
are made—let the blow fall upon whom it may,
you would see that the honor of the Government
was guarded and the laws enforced.

Grant and the Whiskey Ring

It is truly painful to write thus—but viewing the great stake—the means—the ways—the desperation—to thwart justice—even by dragging in their shameful schemes—the names of innocent and dead. Duty requires that you be kept advised—even at the expense of tireing.

I have the honor to be

Respectfully and assuredly

Your Friend

To   W. D. W. Barnard.

The President.

Upon the back of this letter, which is printed without correction of Barnard's somewhat eccentric spelling and punctuation, Grant wrote the famous indorsement,

"Let no guilty man escape."

A later chapter is to be added to the history of the Whiskey Ring. It relates to a statement made by Grant when he was dying. Judge David P. Dyer, of the United States District Court, talking of the national scandal of forty years ago, said for publication now:

"General Grant had no knowledge of the existence of the Whiskey Ring when the prosecutions began, and therefore was not in the remotest manner a party to or in any wise connected therewith. His great mistake was in trusting men who did know, and were parties thereto, and this after their connection with the ring was a matter of common information. Grant was an honest man

133

and implicitly trusted those he believed to be his friends."

As United States district attorney, Judge D. P. Dyer conducted the investigation from beginning to end, and brought about the exposure of this monumental scheme to defraud. Every particle of evidence presented to the grand jury and introduced at the trials in court passed through the hands of Judge Dyer. Furthermore, a mass of confidential information which did not reach the public came into the possession of the district attorney before and after the trials in court. This threw a great deal of light upon the ramifications of the stupendous conspiracy, which had for its object the depletion of the public treasury and the enriching of the conspirators. "At no time during the prolonged inquiry, and in the years since," Judge Dyer said, "was anything discovered that reflected upon General Grant's integrity." But when almost a decade had passed; when sentences had been served, and when the great scandal had passed into history, there came a sequel which brought out in clear light the truth about Grant and the Whiskey Ring, as it never before had been presented.

Judge Dyer tells it. After the conviction of many, and the acquittal of Babcock, Bristow was practically forced out of the Secretaryship of the Treasury, for his aggressive prosecution of those accused. He then went to New York and began the practice of law. The style of his firm was

Grant and the Whiskey Ring

Bristow, Burnett, Peet & Opdyke. General Grant, after his retirement from the Presidency on the 4th of March, 1877, took up his residence also in the City of New York. Grant and Bristow, in a public place, met face to face. Grant saw Bristow, but without the slightest sign of recognition turned his back upon him and walked away. The action was deliberate. It cut Bristow to the quick. Years later Judge Dyer was in New York. He called upon General Bristow, finding him high up in an office building in front of a wood fire in genuine Kentucky comfort. The face of the former Secretary of the Treasury lighted up as he recognized his visitor, and after hearty greetings and the passing of commonplace remarks, General Bristow said: "Colonel Dyer, I have something to tell you that you will be glad to hear. While General Grant was hopelessly ill in his residence in New York, and before he was taken to Mt. McGregor, I received a note from him asking me to call and see him. I showed the note to Mrs. Bristow. Remembering, as she did, the public insult given me by General Grant, she protested against my going. I said to her, 'General Grant was my chief and made me a member of his cabinet. He has sent for me. He has not long to live and I must go and see him.' I went to his house and was shown to his room. I found him sitting in an invalid's chair with wrappings about his neck. He greeted me kindly, and said, 'General Bristow, I wanted to see you for the purpose of acknowledging that I have done you wrong and greatly misjudged you. I believed that in the prosecution of General Babcock and others you and those with whom you were associated were actuated by motives of enmity towards me and my administration. I was wrong and you were right.'

"These were the words of General Grant, as General Bristow, with much feeling, repeated them to me," said Judge Dyer. "To my mind no braver thing was ever done by General Grant in his illustrious life than this acknowledgment to General Bristow. General Grant believed in the innocence of Babcock. He gave his deposition, which was read at the trial; and it was that deposition and the comment of the court upon it, that influenced the jury's verdict. When and how General Grant came to see that he had been deceived by false friends he did not state. I have felt long that this incident stated ought to be given publicity in some permanent form. Grant and Bristow are both dead. They were great men."

Grant and the Third Term

Grant and the Third Term

The movement to nominate General Grant in
1880 for a third term found its earliest support in
St. Louis. It was championed insistently by the
Globe-Democrat with all of the vigor at the command of the editor, Joseph B. McCullagh. The
Republican organization of Missouri, under the
leadership of Chauncey I. Filley, was committed
early to the movement and sent a delegation
bound by the most positive instructions to vote
for Grant. One of the thirty delegates broke
away and voted for Washburne, but twenty-nine
were recorded from first to last for Grant.

On the contrary the anti-third term movement
was formally started in St. Louis. A national
convention was held in Masonic hall and an
address to the country voicing opposition to the
nomination of Grant was issued. This convention was preceded by a mass meeting which filled
to the doors, Mercantile Library hall, the princi-
pal auditorium of St. Louis at that time. The
meeting was held on the 12th of March. A resolution was adopted declaring it is the sense of this
meeting that the nomination of a Presidential
candidate for a third term is inexpedient and
likely to endanger the success of the Republican
party.

The call for a national anti-third term convention followed the mass meeting. On the 6th of
May the delegates assembled in Masonic hall.
John B. Henderson presided. One of the princi-
pal addresses was delivered by Bluford Wilson,

who had been solicitor of the Treasury during the Whiskey Ring prosecutions. Henry Hitchcock of St. Louis was chairman of the committee on resolutions.

It was noteworthy that in none of the addresses at the mass meeting and at the convention was anything said derogatory of the personal character of General Grant. A third term was opposed vigorously, but upon the broad ground that it was against the traditions and not in accord with the spirit of the government of the United States.

Not long before the nominating convention met in June, 1880, Grant wrote to Henry White: "I would not accept a nomination (to a third term) if it were tendered, unless it were to come under such circumstances as to make it an imperative duty—circumstances not likely to arise."

During the National Republican convention in Chicago, 306 delegates voted thirty-six times for Grant, but the anti-third term sentiment was too strong for them. What Grant really thought of the third term movement was not known until many years afterwards when personal letters became public. In 1875-6 Grant stopped a movement to nominate him for a third term immediately following his second by writing a most positive prohibition. In 1878, while he was on his tour around the world, the third term suggestion was renewed and a message was sent through a relative. Grant replied, writing from Rome:

Grant and the Third Term

"It is very kind in Mr. Clark and the gentlemen associated with him to send the message you convey from them; but they must recollect that I had the harness on for sixteen years and feel no inclination to wear it again. I sincerely hope that the North will so thoroughly rally by next election as to bury the last remnant of secession proclivities, and put in the executive chair a firm and steady hand, free from Utopian ideas purifying the party that elected him out of existence."

Even stronger in expression of his position was the letter which Grant wrote to Conkling of New York as the time drew near for the convention. He said:

"There have been exigencies that warranted a second term, but I do not believe that the best interests, or the country's good ever demanded a third term, or ever will. I had my doubts even as to the desirability of a second term, and you know that I have so expressed myself to you in our confidential talks. This is a big country, full of brainy and ambitious men, who can serve the country eminently well as its President, and I sincerely question the policy of thwarting their noble ambition. I feel that our country has amply repaid me for all my services by the honors which it has bestowed upon me, and I feel that to be a candidate or accept the nomination for a third term would be ingratitude, and would eventually affect me with the people who have loved me and whom I love. I am still of the opinion that I should speak to the country; that I should break the silence in a letter declining emphatically to accept a nomination for a third term. I am aware that this matter has gone on to an extent where an announcement from me refusing to accept would be looked upon by some as cowardice. But would it not be far better to be considered a coward than a usurper? I also appreciate your effort in, as you say, the final and supreme effort of your life for supremacy, yet, in the face of all, I still believe that my name should not be presented. And, further, I believe that your anxiety about the effect an announcement from me would have on your future is an error."

The foregoing letter was written to Conkling just a month before the Chicago convention of 1880.

Four times in as many national conventions, the vote of Missouri was cast for Grant. In St. Louis was erected the first monument to him. Two days after the death of the general at Mt. McGregor, President Henry C. Haarstick of the Merchants' Exchange called a meeting of citizens in the great hall. A memorial was adopted. It was hoped that the remains might rest in Bellefontaine, but the family yielded to the solicitations of New York. On the 8th of August, 1885, the day of the obsequies in Riverside Park, a great funeral pageant moved through the streets of St. Louis. Two days later the pageant committee met in the office of the mayor, David R.

Francis, and resolved to form an association "for the purpose of erecting in the City of St. Louis a monument to General Grant." General William T. Sherman, who had taken up his residence in St. Louis, was made president of the association. Mayor Francis and President Haarstick of the Merchants' Exchange were elected vice-presidents. William J. Lemp was chosen treasurer and George H. Morgan secretary. Union and Confederate veterans, Grant men in 1880 and anti-third termers, Republicans and Democrats, joined in the city's tribute. On the 25th of October the statue, Bringhurst's conception, was unveiled on the Twelfth street market place where Grant had sold cordwood.

In the morning of Tuesday, the 6th of May, 1884, Grant thought he was a rich man. His son Buck had gone into partnership with a smooth-spoken young New Yorker, Ferdinand Ward. The general had invested about $200,000 and had allowed his name to be used. He had received large sums which Ward alleged to be profits of the business. Before night of that May day, Grant knew that not only had he lost all, but that others had suffered. He wrote to his relatives: "Financially the Grant family is ruined for the present by the most stupendous frauds ever perpetrated." Grant stripped himself of everything to pay some of the obligations. The Grant farm at St. Louis was one of the assets transferred. It sold for $60,000.

Grant and the Third Term

To leave something for his family, Grant began the writing of his Memoirs. He finished the book on the 1st of July, 1885, and died on the 23rd of July. The Memoirs yielded in royalties over $525,000.

Soon after the Grant & Ward failure, the general said in conversation with a friend: "I have made it the rule of my life to trust a man long after other people gave him up, but I don't see how I can trust any human being again."

As the end approached, Grant, reviewing his career, and answering the question whether there was anything to regret, said: "No, nothing but being deceived in people."

The Grant Farm Letters

The Grant Farm Letters

In the midst of the desperate campaigning from the Wilderness to Cold Harbor, during the summer of 1864, at the supreme test of his qualities as a commander, Grant looked forward to the time when he would retire to the St. Louis farm and raise colts. He was riding one day with his staff when the army of the Potomac was concentrating for the hard fighting at Cold Harbor. As the party approached Totopotomoy creek, they came upon a teamster whipping his horses. The man was swearing and striking one of the horses in the face with the butt-end of his heavy whip. Grant galloped up in front of the teamster, raised his fist and demanded: "What does this conduct mean, you scoundrel? Stop beating those horses." The teamster made an insolent answer and struck the horse again. Grant shook his fist at the teamster, called up an officer and said: "Take this man in charge, and have him tied up to a tree for six hours as a punishment for his brutality."

The incident is told by General Horace Porter, who, as a member of the staff, was present. It is said to be one of only two or three occasions during the war when Grant showed anger. That night while at dinner with his staff, the general referred to the scene with the teamster and said, as General Porter recalled the conversation:

"If people knew how much more they could get out of a horse by gentleness than by harshness, they would save a great deal of trouble both to the horse and to the man. A horse is a particularly intelligent animal. He can be made to do almost anything if his master has intelligence enough to let him know what is required. Some men, for instance, when they want to lead a horse forward, turn toward him and stare him in the face. He, of course, thinks they are barring his way, and he stands still. If they would turn their back to him and move on he would naturally follow. I am looking forward longingly to the time when I can end this war and can settle down on my St. Louis farm and raise horses. I love to train young colts and I will invite you all to visit me and take a hand in the amusement. When old age comes on, and I get too feeble to move about, I expect to derive my chief pleasure from sitting in a big arm chair in the center of a ring— a sort of training course—holding a colt's leading-line in my hand, and watching him run around the ring."

Until his death in the fall of 1874, C. W. Ford represented Grant at St. Louis in a business way. He was the local manager of the Adams Express Company. He had known Grant at the time the lieutenant was stationed at Sackett's Harbor. Their admiration for good horses had drawn the two men together. A strong intimacy had grown in the twenty years' acquaintance. Ford was appointed collector of internal revenue. At frequent intervals he drove out to the Grant farm and saw that the superintendent carried out the instructions of the owner. When Grant visited St. Louis

Ford's team was at his disposal. To John F. Long, another old St. Louis friend, and a neighbor on the Gravois road, the President wrote this letter, which is in the archives of the Missouri Historical Society:

EXECUTIVE MANSION

Washington, D. C., Oct. 25th, 1873.

Dear Judge:

Our old friend Ford is gone! It was just the day week before his death that I met him in Toledo, Ohio, where he had gone expressly to meet me. He looked and seemed as well then— and as cheerful too—as I had ever seen him. I had known Ford from 1851, at which time I was a 1st Lt. 4th Infy., stationed at Sackett's Harbor, N. Y., where he then resided, a young lawyer beloved by all who knew him. For some reason I then formed an attachment for him which has never changed. I trust he bore from this world, to a better, the same good feeling toward me. I know he did; for from the time I was a Lieut. through the time of my farming experience in St. Louis Co., my later military duties, and present duties, he has been the same welcome visitor; he himself never having changed a tone of familiar acquaintance towards me during all this period, and it is certain I never did towards him. He was noble, generous, true & honest. His sacrifices in this life have all been to help others.

The Grant Farm Letters

I started to write something very different—of a business nature connected with Ford's last visit to me, but when I came to write his name could not do so. The subject must be deferred for another occasion.

My kindest regards to you & yours,

Very truly,

Judge J. F. Long,   U. S. Grant.

St. Louis, Mo.

For some time before his death Ford was much troubled about the Whiskey Ring. That he had knowledge of the frauds there was no doubt. The evidence taken at the trials did not show that the collector received part of the fund. Several witnesses testified that they saw money put in an envelope and were told it was for the collector. No one of them saw the money delivered. Before McDonald was appointed supervisor, Ford protested against the appointment. Subsequently he joined those who endorsed it. In his revelations of the "Secrets of the Great Whiskey Ring" McDonald asserted that Ford was a member of the ring. Ford's friends did not believe he received money but held to the theory that he was deceived by McDonald with the argument that the money was needed for campaign purposes and that the people at Washington were consenting to the frauds. In the fall of 1874 information was laid before the collector to the effect that the extent of the frauds was known and that exposure in the near future was inevitable. Ford left the city, went to Chicago, stopped with a friend who was a railroad official and was found dead in his room the next morning.

Before the new collector was appointed three principals in the Whiskey Ring went to the office one Sunday and destroyed records which were evidence of frauds. The collector appointed to succeed Ford was indicted the next year and sent to prison. Fred W. Mathias preceded Ford in the internal revenue service at St. Louis, resigning in June, 1869. Ford was one of the early appointees of Grant after he became President. Mathias said that Ford was an honest man but yielded to the leaders in the conspiracy on the plea that the money was to be used to re-elect Grant. As the conspiracy widened and there was less and less pretense of political purpose in the frauds, Ford became alarmed and determined to know whether Grant understood what was going on. He sought the President and, according to Mr. Mathias, said to him: "General, I suppose you know what we are doing in St. Louis and that it is all right?" Grant's reply was such that Ford realized he had no conception of what was going on and did not enlighten him. Very soon after this, the death of Ford at Chicago was announced. "The fact was," said Mathias, "that Grant was surrounded by men on the make who kept all knowledge of these matters from him."

Perhaps no revelation of the Whiskey Ring

shocked Grant more than that relating to Ford.
When the President's deposition in the Babcock
case was taken questions about Ford were asked
and were answered with emphasis:

"Speaking of C. W. Ford, I presume, General,
that your confidence in him continued up to the
time of his death?

"I never had a suspicion that anything was
wrong.

"Did you preserve letters that you received from
him?

"No sir, I did not preserve them. We corresponded regularly. I had such confidence in him
that I left him to conduct my own affairs there.
And I had to be constantly sending him money.
I would send checks to him of $500, $1,000 and
$1,200 at a time, and he would pay out the money
and account to me for it. My confidence in him
was such that I did that without even saving my
letters."

After the death of Ford, Judge John F. Long,
who had received a Federal appointment, undertook to exercise supervision of the farm. A
change of superintendents was made. Elrod, who
had managed the farm several years, retired.
The place was given to Nat Carlin, who had been
in the employ of the Adams Express Company
and to whom Ford had given a general letter of
recommendation. The President carried on correspondence direct with Carlin, giving him definite and detailed instructions about the farm.

The Grant Farm Letters

He wrote occasionally to Judge Long. Most of these letters were upon the White House stationery. There was no dictation. Every word was in the handwriting of the President. The letters show that Grant had definite and decided views as to tillage, but that his chief interest was in the breeding of horses. They make it evident the general still held to the hope he had expressed in the last year of the Civil War, that after his public life he might retire to the St. Louis farm and raise colts.

When these letters about the farm management were written, the President was in the stormiest period of his eight years in the White House. Some of the highest officers of the government were involved in scandals. There had been changes in the cabinet. A reform wave in protest against existing conditions at Washington was sweeping the country. In the President's own party there was revolt on the part of those who feared that Grant might be induced to submit his name for another term, as some of his friends were then urging. In the midst of such turmoil Grant wrote these letters to the farm. He wrote with a fluency and fullness in striking contrast with his habit of speech. General Horace Porter, who came to know Grant with an intimacy that perhaps no other writer has shown, described the general's method of composition and manner of writing:

"Whatever came from his pen was grammati-

153

cally correct, well punctuated, and seldom showed an error in spelling. In the field he never had a dictionary in his possession and when in doubt about the orthography of a word, he was never known to write it first on a separate slip of paper to see how it looked. He spelled with heroic audacity, and 'chanced it' on the correctness. While in rare instances he made a mistake in doubling the consonants where unnecessary, or in writing a single consonant where two were required, he really spelled with great accuracy. He wrote with the first pen he picked up and never stopped to consider whether it was sharp-pointed or blunt-nibbed, good or bad.

"His powers of concentration of thought were often shown by the circumstances under which he wrote. Nothing that went on around him, upon the field or in his quarters, could distract his attention or interrupt him. Sometimes when his tent was filled with officers, talking and laughing at the top of their voices, he would turn to his table and write the most important communications. There would then be an immediate 'Hush!' and abundant excuses offered by the company; but he always insisted upon the conversation going on, and after awhile his officers came to understand his wishes in this respect, to learn that noise was apparently a stimulus rather than a check upon his flow of ideas, and to realize that nothing short of a general attack along the whole line could divert his thoughts from the subject upon which his mind was concentrated. In writing, his style was vigorous and terse with little ornament. His work was performed swiftly and uninterruptedly, but without any marked display of nervous energy. His thoughts flowed as freely from his mind as the ink from his pen. He was never at a loss for an expression and seldom interlined a word or made a material correction."

One of the Grant farm letters in Mr. Bixby's collection is a curiosity in form. It was written on the two sides of a plain envelope. The Grant family, in accordance with custom, was spending part of the summer at Long Branch on the Jersey coast. Apparently having no stationery at hand, the President picked up this envelope and wrote his wishes to Judge Long. He covered the front of the envelope and, turning it over, filled out the flaps of the reverse. The purpose of this letter was to have Butcher Boy shipped from St. Louis to Washington. Butcher Boy was a fast pacing horse that had been in General Grant's possession eight years and had been sent out from Washington to the farm.

Grant had fourteen horses when he bought Butcher Boy. That purchase was another in the long series of horse stories associated with him. The general had returned to Washington from a trip to the West in October, 1865, after the war. He was riding from his office in the War Department to his home for dinner one day, when a boy in shirt sleeves flashed past driving a little white horse to a cart. Grant turned and looked. The horse went out of sight while the general marveled. Washington was not so large but that the little white pacer could be located. The owner was a butcher. When he learned that the lieutenant-general had taken a fancy to his homely pony, the butcher thought a good deal more of the horse for which he had paid only $76. Grant gave $300 and named his new favorite "Butcher Boy."

The great interest which the President took in the farm is shown by the money he expended as well as by these letters of detailed instructions. The letters are printed as written, without change of spelling or punctuation. About the end of 1874, Grant wrote: "I have already paid out this year some $12,000 on the farm and have not got the means to go further." But at that time he had no intention to abandon his often expressed hope of making it the place of retirement for old age, for he added: "When I go out in the spring I may make arrangements to put the place on a good footing." Spring brought the exposure of the Whiskey Ring and the general's plans for his future underwent radical change.

The Grant Farm Letters

Washington, D. C., Oct. 27th, 1873.

Dear Sir:

When Mr. Ford was in Toledo I gave him a memorandum of what I wished done at the farm. It will be impossible now to repeat. I will however make arrangements through Judge John F. Long, of St. Louis to pay up the carpenters for their work, and all other debts on the farm.

You are at liberty to sell all the calves you can, at good prices, and also cows from time to time. You may take as many horses to board and exercise as you can attend to. It is my intention to get out of cattle entirely in the spring. I authorized Mr. Ford also to buy from the cattle yards one hundred car loads of manure.

My instructions have always been to get the farm all in grass and to purchase grain. This I want still to be done.

Mr. F. also spoke of two mares you wished to purchase. If you can sell cattle, corn or other produce to make the purchase you may do so.

I think the two-year old bay mare, out of Topsy, should be bred. Colts, horse colts, that you do not think will improve enough by training to pay for the trouble you may keep for farm work or sell at your option.

Unless I should give other directions you may account to, and consult with, Judge Long in matters connected with the farm.

157

In a few days I will write to Judge Long and it is probable he will go down to the farm to see you.

I wrote Mr. Elrod that his connection with the farm would end with this month, but that he was at liberty to occupy any vacant house on the place, except the one he is now in, until he is located.

Yours truly,

U. S. Grant.

Mr. Carlin,
Webster Groves P. O.

The Grant Farm Letters

Washington, D. C., Nov. 28th, 1873.

Dear Sir:

Your letter of the 22d inst. was received yesterday. I will answer it in the order of your inquiries. Mr. Elrod was notified in the summer, or spring, that his services on the farm would not be retained after the fall. He should make efforts to give you full possession without delay. If you have hands to board you will require all the room in the house. The inventory of effects on the farm is not a matter of much importance, as every thing there is required for the use of the farm, or for feeding the stock.

As stated before I do not wish to rent any portion of the farm to any body. I would much prefer the land to lay idle, or run to pasture, to renting it. This applies to G. W. Dent's land as well as mine. I do not see anything at present that I can do for Mr. Elrod. If it was in my power to help him I would do so with pleasure. The best thing for him, it seems to me, is to rent Mr. Tesson's place.

Your dispositon of the manure I approve of. As a rule I favor top dressing. But lands that are to be cultivated there is no way of using manure except to plough under. I would suggest that the land in grass be manured first. If there is any left it may be put on any other land you think best. I want to get the farm in grass as rapidly as pos-

159

sible and cultivate none except as the meadows begin to wear out when they must be cultivated for a year or two before they can be got in order to reset. Put in oats & grass and corn and grass as you propose.

I do not feel disposed to buy fencing material to fence off the meadows as you suggest until the farm pays for it. But the outside fences should be good so as to secure the stock. There is a cross fence in the south wood pasture, separating the burned house from the larger part of that field, and one round the hill field, or orchard, both of which might be removed. That orchard is getting old and might be left in the general pasture.

I directed Elrod to straiten the road along the creek before the rail-road was built so as to have the creek in the pasture. Your doing so now I approve of, and it will give you some more rails. You may also make the pond in the north pasture as suggested in your letter. My directions have been for years to use the dead and fallen timber for fire wood and for burning lime, and to clear out all the wood land to about the thickness timber should be left to grow, leaving standing the most desirable varieties of timber.

You may train Beauty and then sell her to the best advantage you can. I am glad you are arranging to turn the stallions out this winter. It is a wonder to me that young Hambletonian is alive now with the care—or lack of care—that he has gone through with. You had better breed the bay two-year old mare in the spring. All the other colts you may try as they get old enough, and the fillies that you think will not pay for training you may set to breeding, and the horse colts you may sell when you can do so to advantage, or keep them for farm work if needed. I will send you two very fine mares next summer, possibly more. One, a sister to Young Hambletonian, is now with foal to Messenger Duroc, probably the most valuable horse in America. The other is a Knox mare, and will be stinted to Jay Gould, a horse that has trotted in 2.21 ½, before she goes out. I will send this letter to the care of Judge Long. But let me know in your next where I am to address you hereafter. I shall be obliged probably to get some one else to take the Judge's place which I am very sorry for.

Yours truly,

[N. Carlin, Esq.,   U. S. Grant.
  Webster Groves P. O.]

The Grant Farm Letters

Washington, D. C., March 8th, 1874.

Dear Sir:

In my last letter I forgot to say anything in answer to your questions in regard to the two stallions on the farm. So far as Peacemaker's pedigree is concerned I can get it reviewed from the gentleman—Mr. Sanford—who raised him. Young Hambletonian was sired by Iron Duke, now owned, and always owned, in Orange Co., N. Y. And almost on the adjoining farm to his sire, old Hambletonian. The full pedigree of Iron Duke can be got—if you have not got it—from the Turf Register. Hambletonian's dam was a very fast and stylish mare—Addie—that I got in 1865. She was the full sister of one of the best stallions in Massachusetts—where both were raised—but I do not know the name of the stallion nor do I recollect his owner's name. If I knew either, the pedigree of the dam would be easily obtained. Addie was a dark bay—not a white spot on her—of great speed and high carriage. Her full brother is a sorrel with white face and two or three white legs. This accounts for the color of Hambletonian, he being from a bay sire as well as dam.

Now that the "fence law" has gone into effect, and the Spring promises to be an early one, might you not have Dr. Sharp's place put in oats & clover? If it can be done, even by a few days hire of extra teams, I think I would do it.

Yours &c

N. Carlin, Esq.   U. S. Grant.

The Grant Farm Letters

Washington, D. C., Apl. 14th, 1874.
Dear Sir:

Your letter announcing the arrival of Richard with the six mares is received. Of the four that went from here one is an old thoroughbred race mare, raised in Virginia not far from here, whose pedigree and performance can, no doubt, be easily obtained. The two mares taken in at Pittsburg are mother and colt. The mother is supposed to be thoroughbred, but her pedigree cannot be obtained. She was raised in the South. Her colt was sired by a Yellow Mexican Saddle horse I had, of great beauty, but not blooded of course. Enclosed I send you all I know of the largest of the three black mares. The other two are Black Hawk Morgan's, no doubt sire and dam. They are too small to breed from to get anything extra, but if they have colts they should make good durable roadsters. I would breed them to the bay stallion. I presume you will breed Topsy's three-year old colt? If there is any promise in Jennie's three-year old I would develop it. Otherwise breed her too. You are aware that she was sired by Young Hambletonian when but two years old.

Your statement for Feby. & March was received. I would like expense account to be given with the same detail that you give receipts— same as given in your previous statements. Soon

163

you will have pasture for all but the work horses so that most of the expense of purchasing feed will be cut off. I hope that hereafter we will be able to raise enough.

Yours truly,

U. S. Grant.

Nat. Carlin, Esq.

The Grant Farm Letters

Washington, D. C., June 7th, 1874.

Dear Sir:

As I have not heard from you recently I write to make some enquiries and to make one or two conditioned suggestions. First, I would like to know how you have the farm planted this season: the condition of crops, fruit, &c. Next, I would ask the condition of the stock, how the mares have been bred, whether they are supposed to be in foal, &c. If you have any two-year old fillies I think I would breed them. If Jennie's three-year old colt (filly) does not promise good speed I would breed her to Peace Maker (proper name Claymore). If she is likely to be fast I would prefer keeping her as an advertisement for Hambletonian and for my own use when she is older. Hambletonian's sister has a filly colt by Messenger Duroc and will be stinted to him again. I am anxious to get a horse colt from her to add to the stock of the farm. She is large and the horse large and the sire of some of the fastest trotting horses now living. Would it not be well to put in this fall as much wheat and timothy as you can find ground suitable to grow timothy upon? There is no use to attempt to raise grass on poor soil. Has lime been tried on any of the fields? If so with what success?

Yours truly,

N. Carlin, Esq.   U. S. Grant.

165

The Grant Farm Letters

(On front side of plain white envelope.)

Long Branch, N. J., July 20th, 1874.

Dear Judge:

Being reduced down to a pair of carriage horses and one saddle horse I have made arrangements for the shipment of Butcher Boy if

(Reverse side of envelope.)

he is still serviceable as a buggy horse, with good care. Will you do me the favor to send this down to the farm, at my expense and tell Carlin to deliver the horse to Adams Ex. Co. for shipment without delay

(1)

unless the horse is becoming decrepid from old age. If I get him here I will keep him

(2)

as long as he and I live.

Yours truly,

U. S. Grant.

[Judge John F. Long,
St. Louis, Mo.]

166

The Grant Farm Letters

Washington, D. C., Nov. 29th, 1874.

Dear Judge:

I hasten to return your letter of the 27th to Carlin just received and read by me. I am too busy—having but just commenced my message to Congress to write at length, but wish to say that the business directions to Carlin I approve of. But there is an impression you have—and which you necessarily took from one of my letters—which does Carlin injustice and which I will correct. Carlin did not say that six hundred dollars would pay his present debts nor did he specify any amount. He said to me that there were four bills which ought to be paid at once, and proceeded to give the amounts of each and to whom due, the figuring I did in my head from memory when I came to write. I cannot say even that he left me under the impression that there were no more bills. The fact is he had turned over to him the farm and stock with nothing to sell but the cattle and a few pigs, and not enough to feed the balance until a new crop could be raised; with correction your instructions are timely and good. In the course of a few days I will send you a check for $1000.00. Should more be necessary to pay up my taxes and indebtedness elsewhere I will send it. I want Carlin also to pick up during the winter four or five more brood mares when he can do so on favorable terms. I will forward you means from time to time to meet his bills. Ford made the contract with Carlin.

The Grant Farm Letters

The amount agreed upon was as I understood it, $800.00 per annum. He finding everything himself except he has the house to live in and necessarily gets his fuel from the farm. The man who goes in the spring gets $600.00 with fuel. In addition I allow him a liberal garden plot with team and time to do the plowing. The balance of the work is done out of his own time." x x x x x

Yours truly,

[Judge John F. Long,   U. S. Grant.
St. Louis, Mo.]

The Grant Farm Letters

Washington, D. C., Dec. 26th, 1874.

Dear Sir:

Enclosed I send you a letter from Mr. Akers, of Lawrence, Kansas. I have written to Mr. A. saying that I would enclose his letter to you and authorize you to select from among the stallions that he wishes to dispose of one to keep on my place the next season. I will make the terms with Mr. Akers. You might select about eight mares to breed to his horse and continue the rest with our own. If you have an opportunity to sell Hambletonian in the spring you might sell him, or dispose of him something on the terms I will take a horse from Mr. A. I am glad to hear that the horses and colts are doing so well. I repeat, if the mares you are driving are likely to make a good team I would continue driving them. If they are not likely to fulfill your expectations then breed them.

I really am not able to send you the articles you ask for. I have already paid out this year some $12,000.00 on the farm and have not got the means to go further. When I go out in the spring I may make arrangements to put the place on a good footing.

Yours truly,

N. Carlin, Esq.

U. S. Grant.

P. S. Write to Mr. Akers on receipt of this.

The Grant Farm Letters

Washington, Apl. 24th, 1875.

Dear Sir:

Your letter of the 12th only reached me on the 22d, probably owing to my absence during the greater part of the time between these dates. In regard to asking Mr. Sprague to send the horse Rhode Island to my farm I cannot do it. If he does not send at the request of Mr. Akers he need not go. I regret to learn the missing of so many foals. I had hoped to get a few more colts from Jennie. She is only eighteen years old. Do you think the smallest black mare is in foal?

In regard to the cows on the place I wish you would turn over one of them to Mr. Jackson. The remainder you can take on the terms contained in your letter. Let me know how many colts we are likely to have this year.

Yours &c.

U. S. Grant.

N. Carlin, Esq.

The Grant Farm Letters

Long Branch, N. J., Aug. 12th, 1875.

Mr. Nat. Carlin, Supt. of Stock in White Haven Farm, Mo., will please deliver to the order of the Hon. J. R. Jones, of Chicago, Ill., my gray gelding Butcher Boy.

U. S. Grant.

The Grant Farm Letters

Custom House, Port of St. Louis,
Surveyor's Office, Oct. 13th, 1875.

Natl. Carlin, Esq.

I am just in receipt of President Grant's letter of the 12th inst. in which he directs me to carry out his instructions given me in my office on the 26th ult: to close out all his personal property on the farm, and to rent or lease out the Farm—and to give possession upon perfecting the Lease.

Hence I advise you that I shall sell all remaining property on the farm (included in the schedule you furnished the Prest.) on Tuesday next the 19th inst. And that from the 20th inst. your services on the farm will cease. Your personal services will be paid for to that date.

Very truly yours,

John F. Long,
Spl. Agent for
U. S. Grant.

Printed in the United States
124470LV00002B/181-198/P

9 781557 090850